"Why have you been following me all this time?" Clint asked.

The young man shrugged, shoveled bacon and beans into his mouth.

"It seemed like a good way to get to know you," he said. "Just watchin' you."

"If you wanted to get to know me, why not just ask?"

"I got a question for you."

"Why'd you let me follow you all that time?"

"I doubled back on you a few times, tried to catch you," Clint said. "You were too good."

"Was I?"

"Where did you learn that?"

"From an old Indian."

The young man drank some coffee. "But you never tried to lose me?"

"I figured you must have a reason for what you were doing," Clint said.

"I did," he said. "I do."

THE GUNSMITH

385

THE SILENT DEPUTY

J. R. ROBERTS

JOVE BOOKS, NEW YORK

THE BERKLEY PUBLISHING GROUP
Published by the Penguin Group
Penguin Group (USA) LLC
375 Hudson Street, New York, New York 10014

USA • Canada • UK • Ireland • Australia • New Zealand • India • South Africa • China

penguin.com

A Penguin Random House Company

THE SILENT DEPUTY

A Jove Book / published by arrangement with the author

For information, address: The Berkley Publishing Group,
a division of Penguin Group (USA) LLC,
375 Hudson Street, New York, New York 10014.

ISBN: 978-0-515-15442-9

PUBLISHING HISTORY
Jove mass-market edition / January 2014

PRINTED IN THE UNITED STATES OF AMERICA

10 9 8 7 6 5 4 3 2 1

Cover illustration by Sergio Giovine.

ONE

The Stalker was still there.

It had been months since Clint had first seen the rider on his trail, and he had still not been able to get a good look at the man. In Louisiana, several weeks ago, he believed the man had saved him from a flood by providing a boat. But since he'd left Louisiana, the man was still there and had gotten no closer. He'd tried several times to circle around him, or lie in wait for him, but in each case he'd failed. He was actually looking forward to meeting the man, but it was clear that would have to happen when the Stalker was ready.

He didn't think the man wanted to kill him. He'd had too many opportunities to do that—the least of all being when he could have simply left Clint to drown. So what he had to do was wait—wait for the man to make up his mind if and when he wanted them to meet.

Clint was actually looking forward to meeting the man because he was so good at what he was doing.

* * *

The Stalker knew it was time. This had gone on long enough. He'd observed the Gunsmith for a long time, thought he knew what kind of man he was.

It was time for him to find out if he was right.

Clint camped, built a fire after seeing to Eclipse's need, and put on a pot of coffee before laying some strips of bacon in his frying pan. After a while he added the beans. He was eating when Eclipse shifted nervously, but Clint had already heard the movements out in the dark.

"I know you're out there!" he called. "I've got enough coffee, bacon, and beans for two."

He waited to see if there'd be a response, then he heard the movement again—a man walking a horse. Before long, they came into the light.

"Come ahead," Clint said. "You've been on my trail so long I feel like we're friends."

The man approached and Clint was surprised at how young he was. He was fairly accomplished for someone of his age.

"See to your horse," Clint said. "I'll pour you some coffee."

The young man nodded, walked his horse over to where Clint had picketed Eclipse. When he returned to the fire, Clint handed him a plate and a cup of coffee. The young man sat across the fire from him.

"That was you, wasn't it?" he asked. "In Louisiana? You left the boat outside the house?"

"Yes."

"How did you escape the flood?"

"There was a canoe with the boat," he said. "I took that."

"You saved my life."

"So I did."

"Why?"

"Didn't see any point in lettin' you die."

"Why have you been following me all this time?" Clint asked.

The young man shrugged, shoveled bacon and beans into his mouth.

"It seemed like a good way to get to know you," he said. "Just watchin' you."

"If you wanted to get to know me, why not just ask?"

"I got a question for you."

"What?"

"Why'd you let me follow you all that time?"

"I doubled back on you a few times, tried to catch you," Clint said. "You were too good."

"Was I?"

"Where'd you learn that?"

"From an old Indian."

The young man drank some coffee. "But you never tried to lose me?"

"I figured you must have a reason for what you were doing," Clint said.

"I did," he said. "I do."

"What are they?"

The young man shook his head.

"Not yet," he said.

"Why come walking into my camp now?" Clint asked.

The man looked at Clint, chewing, and said, "Guess I was hungry."

"Do I get to know your name?"

The young man seemed to consider that question for

a few moments, then said, "Travis. Can I have some more coffee?"

He held his cup out and Clint filled it.

"Travis," he said.

"Uh-huh."

"Is that your real name?"

Travis just looked at him.

"Okay," Clint said. "For now, you're Travis."

"Can I call you Clint?'

"Why not?" Clint asked. "After all, we've known each other all this time."

TWO

They sat at the fire and drank coffee in silence for a few minutes.

"Look," Clint said finally, "you're kind of young for us to have a history that I don't remember. Is there somebody else in your family I might know? Is that what this is about?"

"Not really."

Clint studied the gun on the young man's hip. It was not new, but also not well worn. It looked like the kind of gun someone might have gotten as a present, or something he might have inherited. It was not a gunman's gun.

But the young man had talents. From an old Indian? Or inherited from someone?

"So what now?" Clint asked. "Tomorrow you go back to trailing me?"

"No," Travis said, "I thought maybe I'd ride along with you for a change."

"That would be a change," Clint agreed, "but why should I agree?"

"Curiosity."

"That's all?"

"If there's one thing I've learned from watchin' you," Travis said, "it's that you're a curious man."

"Is that all you've learned?"

"No," Travis said, "there's a lot of other things, but that's all I wanna talk about tonight."

"How safe am I supposed to feel going to sleep with you in camp?" Clint asked.

"Don't you think if I wanted to kill you, I would have tried by now?" Travis asked. "Maybe even succeeded by now?"

"Well," Clint said, "tried anyway."

Travis actually laughed, handed his empty plate across to Clint.

"More?" Clint asked.

"No," Travis said, "you're not that good a cook. And that coffee could be used for a lot of other things—like horse liniment."

"I like my coffee," Clint said. "That's why I make it that way." He stood up. "Well, now, the least you can do to earn your keep is do the dishes."

"Okay," Travis said.

While Travis used dirt to clean the dishes, Clint studied him. He was looking for some resemblance to . . . well, anyone. This had to be somebody's son who had come looking for him. If he was the son of an enemy, why hadn't he tried to kill him? And if he was the son of a friend, why not say so?

They slept on opposite sides of the fire, rolled up in

their bedrolls. Clint slept fitfully, so he was surprised when he awoke the next morning to find daylight.

He sat up, annoyed with himself. The kid could have killed him in his sleep with no problem. And what annoyed him further was that Travis was gone.

Clint stood up. Travis's horse was gone. The young man had probably walked the horse out of camp before saddling him, and riding off. Was Clint supposed to be impressed? He might have been if he wasn't so angry with himself.

He made himself some coffee and brooded while he drank it. He had no appetite, so he doused the fire, saddled Eclipse, and rode out. Initially, he tried to find Travis's tracks, thinking maybe he could follow him, but that old Indian—or whoever it was—had taught the young man well. There were no tracks.

Clint rode along for a while, then stopped and turned in his saddle. Was Travis behind him again? What was the point of coming into camp? Just to prove he could?

In the light from the fire, Travis had looked to be about twenty-two or so to Clint. He wondered how close he was in his estimation. This twenty-two-year-old was certainly playing with his head. If he was back to following Clint, he was keeping out of sight this time, where in the past he was not shy about being seen.

Clint decided not to worry about it. He had at least been given further proof that the young man—whatever his real name—was not looking to kill him. But he did have something on his mind, and he would probably reveal it when he felt the time was right.

Clint continued to ride in the direction of Labyrinth, Texas, where he figured he'd relax and spend some time in his friend Rick Hartman's saloon, Rick's Place. Let young Travis follow him there. Maybe the friendly atmosphere of Labyrinth would rub off on him and loosen his tongue.

Travis felt he had accomplished his goal. He'd gotten a good, close-up look at Clint Adams, learned a bit more about the man, and then made his point by leaving camp without waking the Gunsmith.

Now he'd follow him for a while without letting Adams see him. Let the man wonder about it for a while. Things were pretty much going the way "Travis" had planned.

THREE

Labyrinth, Texas, had not changed. It never did. The town looked the same now as it had the first day Clint had ridden in. That was a lot of years ago, but Labyrinth was happy with its identity.

And Clint was happy with Labyrinth as a place to lie low from time to time. Faces changed—blacksmiths, bartenders, hotel clerks—but the buildings remained the same. And Rick Hartman was always there. He hadn't left town in a very long time, and he preferred it that way.

Clint left Eclipse at the livery stable, handing the horse over to the same man who had been there the last time he'd come to town, a few months before. He remembered that his name was Russell.

"Hey, you're back!" Russell said as Clint walked Eclipse into the stable.

"Well, that certainly makes me feel real welcome," Clint said.

"Oh, I wasn't talkin' to you," the older man said, "I

was talkin' to this handsome feller." He went to Eclipse and stroked the big Arabian's neck. In his sixties, Russell had been working with horses a long time, and Eclipse could feel that.

"I get it," Clint said.

Russell was cooing to Eclipse, stroking his neck. Clint removed his saddlebags and his rifle without interrupting the reunion.

"Any idea how long you're stayin' this time?" Russell asked.

"I don't know," Clint said, "A few days, maybe more."

"Hopefully more."

"Just take good care of him," Clint said.

"Oh, I will."

"And there may be another man riding in behind me," Clint said. "A youngster in his twenties. If he does come in, would you send me a message over at the hotel?"

"I'll do that," Russell said.

"Labyrinth House this time," Clint said.

"Yes, sir."

Clint left the livery, walked over to the hotel, and checked in. The clerk was new, but he must have been informed that Clint came to town from time to time, because he greeted him in a very friendly manner.

Clint left his saddlebags and rifle in his room and walked over to Rick's Place.

"Put a beer on the bar for my returning friend, Henry," Rick said as Clint entered.

"Hey, Rick." The two friends shook hands warmly.

"You've only been gone a few months," Rick said. "What's been going on?"

Clint grabbed the beer and drank some of it to clear his throat of trail dust.

"I've got a story for you," Clint said. "It's kind of interesting."

He went on to tell his friend about "Travis."

"Following you for months?" Rick said. "I'm surprised you put up with that."

"He's good at it," Clint said. "Whoever taught him did a damn fine job."

"So you're impressed with him?"

"Considering his age, yeah, I am."

"And he had the nerve to come walking into your camp," Rick said. "Maybe he's not so impressed with you."

"Maybe not."

"Two more, Henry," Rick said. When the fortyish bartender set them on the bar, he grabbed them. "Let's have a seat."

Clint followed Rick to his regular table in the back. The saloon was sparsely populated in the afternoon, and the gaming tables were still covered. There were also no girls working the floor yet. From this table, Rick could observe the entire place.

He set the two beers down and asked Clint, "So he doesn't look familiar to you?"

"No, he doesn't," Clint said. "I've been trying to figure out if maybe I wronged his parents, but if I did, I don't remember them. Not enough to see them in him anyway."

"You think he followed you here?"

"I know he did," Clint said. "Nothing happened in camp that night that would make him quit."

"And you didn't hear him outside your camp over the next few nights?"

"Not a sound."

"I'm looking forward to meeting this young man," Rick said. "I wonder if he'll have the nerve to come walking in here."

"I don't see why not."

"What else has been going on?"

Clint took the time to tell Rick about some of his adventures, especially surviving the flood on Bayou Teche—thanks to Travis.

"Sure doesn't sound like he means you harm," Rick commented. "I would think the curiosity would be killing you."

"It was for a while," Clint said. "But then I decided it was all up to him. He wants something. Eventually, I'll find out what it is."

"So how long do you figure to stick around this time?" Rick asked.

"Don't know," Clint said, reaching for the fresh beer. "I'll just take it as it comes."

"Got some new girls working," Rick said. "Maybe that'll interest you."

Clint drank some beer and said, "If I'm going to be meeting some new girls, I guess I'd better have a bath."

"We'd all appreciate it," Rick said.

FOUR

Clint finished his beer and went back to his hotel for the bath. He kept his gun close at hand while in the tub. It wasn't because of Travis; it was just something he always did.

After the bath he dressed in fresh clothes, took his dirty trail clothes down to the Chinese laundry, where they knew him.

"You come back to town, Mr. Clint," the Chinaman who ran the place said. Clint could never pronounce the man's name, so they just agreed between them that Clint would think of him as the Chinaman.

"I from China, and I a man," the Chinaman said, "so no insult." He cackled. The man could have been anywhere from forty to sixty. He had a big family working for him in the laundry—his wife and four daughters. No sons.

"But we not finished trying," he'd told Clint once,

cackling again. His wife had a smooth, handsome face, and her age was also difficult to figure, but Clint thought she was well beyond childbearing age.

"How are your girls?" Clint asked.

"They growing up," the Chinaman said. "Pretty like their mama, not ugly like me."

"How old are they?"

"Fourteen, fifteen, sixteen, and eighteen," the man replied. "Too young for you, Mr. Clint."

"I agree," Clint said. "You've got nothing to worry about from me, but I'm sure there are some young men in town who are sniffing around."

"They sniff too close, I chop off sniffer!" the Chinaman said. "I got hatchet."

"I know you do," Clint said. "I'll come back for my clothes tomorrow, if that's all right."

"You take ticket," the Chinaman said, handing Clint a ticket. "You no have ticket, you no get shirt." The Chinaman cackled again.

"I'll see you tomorrow."

"I be here," the Chinaman said. "I always here."

Clint left, thinking that maybe he should try pronouncing the man's name one last time before he left town. Just to show respect.

"Travis" sat on his horse just outside Labyrinth, Texas, wondering how long Clint Adams meant to stay in this small town. During all the time he'd been trailing Adams, the man had never stopped here before.

Using his binoculars he saw that Adams had gone into the hotel, then a saloon called Rick's Place, and then the hotel again. Later he came out and went to a laundry. At that point he decided that Clint Adams meant to stay in Labyrinth for a while.

The Gunsmith would probably expect him to come into town after him. Maybe he would, but he wouldn't do it today. He decided to camp for the night, and maybe he'd ride into town in the morning.

Maybe . . .

Clint waited until it was after dark to return to Rick's Place. Walking from the hotel to the saloon, though, he turned and looked up into the hills east of town. He could see the light of a campfire. It wasn't hard to figure who was camped up there. "Travis" was once again advertising his location. Clint thought about riding up there and surprising the young man in his camp, but decided against it. He was still determined to let the young man call the play.

He turned and entered Rick's Place, looking forward to meeting Rick's new girls.

Rick did not employ whores.

The bulk of his business was whiskey and gambling. The girls he hired were window dressing. Their job was to serve drinks, that's all. Anything else they wanted to do was up to them. Rick was always careful to explain to new girls he hired that there were no cribs or rooms for them to take men to. No "nickel nights" at Rick's Place. If they wanted to do that, there was a whorehouse in town they could work for.

Clint entered and went to the bar. The place was busy. There were other saloons in Labyrinth, but Rick's was the most popular place in town. It had the best beer and whiskey, and honest games.

And pretty girls.

Rick was always careful to hire very pretty girls. Working the floor were a blond, a redhead, and two brunettes, all of whom were pretty, none of whom was thirty.

In the past Rick used to tell the girls to pay special attention to Clint, as he was Rick's good friend. But Clint had put a stop to that.

"If one of these nice young ladies shows interest in me, I'd like it to be because of me, and not because you told them to."

Rick had shrugged and said, "Whatever you want. I was just trying to be helpful."

So Clint stood at the bar with a beer in hand and watched the new girls work the floor.

FIVE

One girl caught Clint's eye.

She was blond and, at maybe twenty-eight or so, older than the other girls. She was tall and lean, except for her breasts, which were impressive. And her trim waist made them look all the more so.

He watched her work the room, gliding effortlessly away from the groping hands of drunk cowboys.

"I see you've zeroed in on the class of the bunch," Rick said, coming up next to him.

"What's her name?"

"Delia."

"How long has she been working here?"

"About a month," Rick said. "She was very pleased to discover we didn't expect her to sell her wares."

"I imagine she'd do very well if she did."

"No doubt," Rick said. "But she's happy just slinging drinks."

"Smart?"

"Very," Rick said. "She's exactly your type, my friend."

"What type is that?"

"You get just what you see," Rick said. "There's no pretense about the girl."

"That's good."

"There's no pretense about you either," Rick said. "I've known that about you from the start."

"I wasn't always like that, but it's the only way I know how to be after all these years," Clint said.

"Well," Rick said, "it looks to me like she's interested. She keeps looking over here."

"Well, you're her boss," Clint said. "She keeps looking at you."

"I don't think it's me," Rick said, "but I'm going to my office to do some paperwork, so you'll find out. I'll see you later."

Clint raised his mug to his friend, who turned and walked to the back of the saloon, entered his office. Clint then glanced over at Delia, and saw her looking at him. When their eyes met, she held his for a long moment, then turned her head.

Clint looked around at the gaming that was going on. He saw faro, roulette, and blackjack, but no poker. He had played the other games, of course, but poker was his preference. At the moment, he had no desire to partake in any of those other games.

But he and Delia were playing a game with each other, tossing glances back and forth. As the night wore on, the glances became hot. Finally, she passed close enough for him to reach out and grab her arm.

"I was wondering when you would make a move," she said frankly.

"Do you know who I am?"

"It doesn't matter," she said. "You're a cut above the rest of them. What are you looking for, sir?"

"Just some time," he said. "Some pleasant time to pass. And you?"

"The same," she said. "I'm not looking for a boyfriend or a husband."

"Seems we're looking for the same thing."

"What hotel are you in?" she asked.

"Labyrinth House."

"What room?"

"Twelve."

"I get off here at two."

"I'll be awake," he said, "reading."

"Ah, you read?" she asked. "Like I said, a cut above."

"I hope you'll still feel that way," he said, "in the morning."

SIX

Clint was reading when there was a knock at the door. He marked his place by folding a page corner and set the book aside. He hoped Mr. Twain would not object.

He walked to the door with his gun behind his back in his left hand. When he opened it, he saw Delia waiting in the hall.

"Miss me?" she asked.

"Terribly."

"That's good to hear. May I come in?"

"Please."

He let her enter, then closed the door, walked to his holster hanging on the bedpost, and slid the gun home.

"Do you always answer the door with a gun?" she asked.

"I do."

"Oh, right," she said. "I did ask about you after you left. I guess the Gunsmith has to be careful, doesn't he?"

"All the time."

"Want to frisk me for a gun?" she asked, raising her hands. She had changed into a dress more suited for walking in the street than the revealing dress she'd been wearing at work.

"Not necessary," he assured her.

When Delia smiled at Clint, it was an invitation that he was more than willing to accept. She stood in front of him with her arms at her sides and a glint in her eye. As he approached her, she reached up to place her hands upon his shoulders and open her mouth just enough for the tip of her tongue to slip out so she could lick her upper lip.

That was all Clint needed to see. He'd had something in mind to say to her, but instead allowed himself to give in to his instincts by grabbing her by the hips and pulling her close. She leaned her head back and let out a grateful breath as Clint tasted the side of her neck. Delia's golden blond hair brushed against his face, and her breasts pressed against his chest. His hands moved along her body, feeling her generous curves through the layers of clothing she wore. Within seconds, he was pulling that clothing off, stripping her bare with a need that grew by the second.

He wasn't the only one that was anxious. Delia's hands were busy as well, unbuckling Clint's belt, pulling his shirt open, and throwing his clothes aside until her fingertips were raking against his naked skin. There was a perfectly good bed nearby, but Clint wasn't about to wait long enough to take the five or six steps required to get there. Instead, he pushed her against the closest wall and reached down for her thigh.

Delia lifted that leg up to wrap it partway around Clint's waist. His cock was already hard and grew even harder when it found the damp patch of hair between her legs. Looking hungrily at him, she ground her hips slowly, rubbing the lips of her pussy up and down along the length of his shaft. Wrapping her arms around the back of his neck, she locked her eyes on him and whispered, "You like that?"

"You know I do."

"There's something I'd like even more."

"Let me guess," Clint said while reaching down to guide himself between her legs. The moment his rigid pole entered her, they both let out satisfied moans. Delia leaned her head back and closed her eyes, smiling as he started pumping in and out of her. Clint reached down with both hands to cup her buttocks, which also allowed him to drive into her with even more force. Every time he thrust his hips, Delia grunted and was pushed against the wall. Her nails dug into his back, and her hips moved with his rhythm.

When Clint lifted her, she wrapped both legs around him and gripped him tightly with them as well as her arms. He wanted to take her to the bed, but when he got halfway there, he could feel Delia's entire body tensing. She leaned back, swaying slightly while her hips ground against him with building force to ride him even harder.

Before long, her eyes snapped open and she stifled a moan as tremors started working through her body. Delia embraced him and gasped into his ear while her climax ran its course, sighing with satisfaction when it was through. Clint then carried her to the bed and set her down. Delia's body glistened with sweat and she barely had the strength to move.

"God, Clint," she gasped. "That was . . . that was . . ."

Smirking, he told her, "I'm not through with you yet."

She lay on the mattress with her legs hanging over the edge. As he moved his hands along her legs, she spread them for him and stretched both arms over her head to grab hold of the blanket beneath her. Clint slipped inside her while pulling her toward him. Delia moaned with approval and gripped the blankets even tighter as he started to thrust in and out.

Clint got a breathtaking view of Delia's full, rounded breasts as he pumped between her long legs. Her large nipples were erect, and when he reached out to cup her breasts, she clasped her hands on top of his to hold them in place. Massaging her tits while burying his thick cock inside her again and again, Clint moved his hands down the front of her body. He savored the smooth texture of her skin while driving into her faster and harder.

Delia moaned loudly, opening her legs wider to accommodate every one of Clint's thrusts. In one last powerful motion, Clint drove in as deep as he could go before exploding inside her. Delia's breathing quickened with another explosion of her own, and when Clint opened his eyes again, he found her looking up at him with a tired smile.

SEVEN

Clint spent the entire night and much of the morning in bed with Delia. He'd been on the trail a long time. A woman was one of the things he had missed, so he made the most of having one in bed with him—and one who was so energetic about it.

He woke up first, saw Delia lying on her back next to him, no sheet on her. Feeling himself stirred by the sight of her, he forced himself out of bed. His stomach was growling, and another thing he had missed while on the trail was a breakfast of steak and eggs.

He washed with the water from the pitcher and basin on the chest of drawers, doing it as quietly as he could, and then got dressed. Before he left, she stirred and rolled over onto her right side, presenting him with a fine view of her ass.

He forced himself out the door.

He walked to a small café that was located halfway

between his hotel and Rick's Place. Sometimes, when he was in Labyrinth, he joined Rick for breakfast at the saloon, prepared in his kitchen. Today, however, he chose to eat alone.

Five men rode into town from the north, moved slowly toward Rick's Place, reined in outside.

"O'Brien," Tom Barry said, "stay here, keep watch, and take care of the horses."

"Sure, boss."

Tom Barry had been hired to do a job. When he was in town a couple of weeks before, he'd spent a lot of time at Rick's Place. He was impressed with the amount of business the saloon did, and had come back with his gang to relieve Rick Hartman of some of his hard-earned cash. Keeping his ears open, he had first heard the name "Hartman," then discovered that the man had a low opinion of banks. To Barry, that meant large sums of money kept on the premises. The saloon and gambling hall was an easier target than a bank.

Barry had ridden out and met with his gang at a pre-arranged place in North Texas. He laid out the job, told them what he knew about Labyrinth . . .

"They got one lawman, a sheriff with no deputies, and the saloon ain't got no security to speak of. One night I saw the bartender break up a fight, and he did it by hisself."

"So what yer stayin' is," Cameron Davis said, "it's easy pickin's."

"The easiest."

"So whatta we waitin' fer?" Tracy Hastings asked . . .

* * *

Barry dismounted, followed by three of his four men. The fifth, Irish O'Brien, remained mounted and kept an eye out for possible trouble.

Barry walked to the front door, his three men behind him. The door was locked, but he'd expected that. He knocked, rather than pounded, as he did not want to attract anyone's attention, except for somebody on the inside.

He knocked again and the door was finally opened by a tall man in his forties, who stared out at them without expression.

"We're closed," he said.

Barry produced his gun and pointed it at the man's face.

"I don't think so," he said. "I think you're open."

The man stared at the gun barrel, still no expression on his face.

"Back away, bartender," Barry said. "We're comin' in."

"That'd be a mistake," the bartender said.

"I don't think so," Barry said, "but let's just see. Back up!"

The man did as he was told. Barry moved in with him, and the other three eased in behind him past the batwings, closing the door again.

"What's this?" Rick Hartman asked.

He was seated at a table with breakfast in front of him. The other tables were either covered, or had chairs stacked on them.

"Just stay nice and relaxed, Hartman," Barry said.

"I know you," Rick said.

"I don't think so."

"Yeah, I don't forget faces," Rick said. "You were in here a week or so ago, more than once. And as I recall, you drank, but didn't gamble."

"You're right," Barry said. "You do have a pretty good memory."

"What's this all about?" Rick asked. "We overcharge you for a beer?"

"No, your prices are just fine," Barry said. "In fact, I think they're so good that you probably have a nice amount of cash lying around somewhere."

"You're right, I do," Rick said. "it's called . . . a bank."

"Nah, nah," Barry said, waving the comment off with the barrel of his gun. "What I heard when I was here is that you don't like banks. Don't trust 'em. I don't blame you. I don't trust 'em either. I like 'em, but I don't trust 'em."

"Well," Rick said, "I guess you heard wrong."

"We'll see," Barry said. "Hey, bartender, I see you tryin' to sneak behind that bar. You make it and you're dead."

Henry, the bartender, stopped.

Barry turned and looked at his men.

"One of you go back there and see what our friend is so anxious to get his hands on."

Cam Davis went behind the bar and reached underneath.

"Well, lookee here," he said, holding a shotgun up. "A Greener. Mean-lookin' thing. This woulda cut you in half, Tom."

Barry gave the man a dirty look. They all had instructions not to mention any names while inside.

"Keep your eye on the bartender," Barry said. He looked at Hastings. "Watch the door." The other man,

Zeke Kane, just leaned against the wall and folded his arms.

"Okay," Barry said, looking at Rick, "let's go."

"Where?"

Barry shrugged.

"Wherever the money is."

"I told you," Rick said. "It's in the bank."

Barry turned to Cam Davis and nodded. Davis moved over and rammed the butt of the shogun into Henry's gut. The bartender doubled over, coughing and clutching his stomach.

"That's not gonna get my money out of the bank for you," Rick said.

Barry looked up at the ceiling.

"Anybody else in the building?" he asked.

"Nope," Rick said, "just me and Henry."

"What about your girls?"

"They don't have rooms upstairs," Rick said. "It's not that kind of place."

"Your dealers?"

"Same thing," Rick said. "They live elsewhere."

"Okay, then," Barry said, "let's go to your office and have a look."

"You're wastin' your time," Rick said.

"We'll see about that," Barry said. To his men he said, "Stay here, watch the bartender and the bar."

"Right . . . boss."

He waved with his gun barrel again and said, "Let's go, Hartman."

EIGHT

Rick led the way to his office door, opened it, and went in.

"Slow," Barry said.

Rick slowed down, stopped.

"Where's the money?" Barry knew Hartman would stick to his story, but he was hoping a glance would give the location away. No luck. Rick Hartman just stared straight ahead.

"Just stand still."

Barry walked to Rick's desk, opened the drawers, found the gun in the top-right-hand one. He took it out and tucked it into his belt, then opened the others. No money.

"Come over here and sit behind your desk."

Rick obeyed, and Barry moved away so the man wouldn't make a grab for his gun.

"Just sit still while I have a look around."

"Look all you want," Rick said.

Barry proceeded to search, knocking books off shelves

in search of a safe. When he got to the file cabinet, he found the drawers locked.

"Key."

This was the first time Rick showed any emotion. He pressed his lips together as he reached into his vest pocket and came out with a key.

"Just put it there on the edge of the desk."

Rick reached out, put the key down.

"Now sit back."

He obeyed.

Barry came forward, grabbed the key, and walked to the file cabinet. Holding his gun in his left hand, he put the key in the lock with his right and turned it. Once the drawers were unlocked, he put the key on top of the cabinet and then started opening them. When he opened the bottom drawer, he saw a cash box.

"Well—" he said, straightening, but in that moment he saw Rick Hartman spring at him and he fired . . .

Out in the saloon they heard the shot and the bartender started to run for the office door.

"Hey, hold it!" Davis yelled.

Kane didn't wait, though. He pushed off the wall, drew his gun, and fired at the bartender's back.

Tom Barry came out of the office, carrying a fistful of cash.

"What happened?" Hastings asked.

"We gotta go," Barry said. "He came at me and I hadda stop him." He stopped short when he saw the bartender. "What happened here?"

"He started running toward the office," Hastings said. "Kane stopped him."

"Is that all the cash there is?" Davis asked.

"I stuffed some in my pockets," Barry said. "Don't know how much we got, but we got to get out of here. We can count it later."

They ran for the front door, opened it, and ran out. O'Brien was holding the reins of all the horses, who were skittish.

"What happened?" he yelled.

"We gotta go!" Barry said.

They started to mount their horses.

"Hey, hold it!" someone yelled.

They turned and saw a man wearing a badge running toward them with his gun out.

"Kill 'im!" Barry shouted.

Hastings was still holding the Greener, so he turned it on the lawman and pulled both triggers.

Clint was only halfway through his steak and eggs when he heard what sounded like shots. He looked around, but none of the other diners seemed to notice. Even the waiter went about his business.

Then somebody definitely let go with both barrels of a shotgun and everybody noticed.

Clint jumped up from his seat and was out the door in seconds, but then he stopped.

Where had the shots come from?

"It's over by the saloon," someone yelled.

"Which saloon?" Clint shouted.

"Rick's!"

Clint started running, got to the front of the saloon in time to see five horsemen riding off. They rounded a corner and were gone before he could get off a shot.

He looked around for a horse, but there wasn't one. It was early, and there were no horses on the street.

Just a man lying in the dirt.

Clint ran over, saw that it was the local lawman. It took only a moment to determine that the man was dead, cut down by a shotgun. He looked at the saloon, saw the door sitting open.

Jesus, he thought, Rick.

He ran for the saloon.

As he entered the saloon, he saw the bartender lying on the floor, bleeding from a wound in his back. He looked around, but didn't see Rick. However, the door to Rick's office was open, so he ran to it and entered. He found his friend on the floor, bleeding from a chest wound.

Alive.

He heard someone come to the door behind him.

"Get the doctor!" he shouted. "Fast."

He looked around for something to use to stanch the flow of blood, finally just took off his own shirt and pressed it to the wound.

He was still holding it there when the doctor arrived.

NINE

Clint was waiting in the outer room of the doctor's office while the sawbones worked on Rick, who was still breathing when they got him there.

"You saved his life by stopping the blood," the doctor said. "Now it's my turn."

"The sheriff and bartender are dead," Clint said. "We need you to keep Rick alive so we can find out who did this."

"Plus," the doctor said, "he's your friend."

"Yes," Clint said, "there's that."

He was still sitting there in the third hour when the door opened and several men walked in. He recognized the mayor, Seth Jackson. The others must have been members of the town council.

Clint stood up.

"How is he?" the mayor asked. In his forties, he was a young politician, newly elected just the year before.

"The doctor is still working on him," Clint said.

"We took the bartender and the sheriff over to the undertaker's," Jackson said. "Do you know these gentlemen?"

"No," Clint said.

"Harry Morgan, Dave Wilder, and George Mahill," Jackson said. "Members of the town council."

"Gents. What can I do for you?"

"Wear this," Jackson said, holding out the sheriff's star.

"Whoa," Clint said, "there's no deputy?"

"No."

"Then hire one," Clint said. "Or better yet, hire a new sheriff."

"That's what we're trying to do right now," Jackson said.

"Not me," Clint said. "Isn't there somebody else?"

"Nobody with your qualifications," Jackson said. "And certainly nobody with your vested interests."

"I know what my interests are," Clint said. "What are yours?"

"Somebody has to track these miscreants down."

"Why?" Clint asked. "Why are you so interested? It's not like they robbed the bank."

"They robbed and shot one of this town's most prominent citizens," Jackson said. "Rick's Place brings a lot of people to this town."

"While they're here," George Mahill said, "they spend money in other places, as well."

"Like George's general store," Harry Morgan said.

"And your hardware store," Mahill said to Morgan.

"Plus the fact that Rick Hartman is also our friend," Dave Wilder said.

Clint didn't know for sure if any of these men were friends with Rick, but certainly the rest of what they said was true.

"Well," Clint said, "I have to tell you all that as soon as I know Rick is out of danger, I do plan on tracking down the men who shot him."

"Good," Jackson said.

"But I'm not going to wear that," Clint added, pointing to the badge.

"Then don't wear it," Mayor Jackson said. "Put it in your pocket. At some point, it's going to come in handy having official standing."

"What kind of official standing will I have after I ride out of the county?"

"A badge is a badge," Jackson said. He held it out to him again.

"Yeah, okay," Clint said, taking it. "I'll put it in my pocket."

"Very good."

A door opened, interrupting them. Dr. Evans stepped out, wiping his hands on a towel.

"How is he?" Clint asked.

"I've done all I can," the doctor said. "I got the bullet out and repaired the damage. Now the rest is up to him."

"When will we know something?" Clint asked.

"Maybe by morning."

The news did nothing to raise Clint's spirits.

"Hey," the doctor said, "he's alive. You've been here a long time. Get something to eat, get some rest. Hell, get a drink."

"Jesus," Clint said, "what happens with the saloon now? Who's in charge?" He looked at the mayor.

"Maybe you and I should talk privately," Jackson said. "Come with me to my office, I'll give you a drink."

Clint looked at the doctor.

"Go," he said. "I'll find you if there's any news."

"Okay," Clint said.

He stepped outside with the mayor and the other members of the council.

"You gents better get back to work," Jackson said. "I have to talk to our new sheriff."

The men grumbled, but left.

"I'm not really the new sheriff, you know," Clint said.

"However you want to look at this is fine with me," the mayor said. "But the fact is, you've got the badge at the moment."

The tin felt heavy in his shirt pocket.

"Come on," Jackson said, "we need to talk."

TEN

Tom Barry signaled his men to stop and reined in his horse about ten miles from town.

"Anybody hit?" he asked.

"I don't think anybody in town got off a shot, boss," Hastings said.

"We're good," O'Brien said.

"Okay, then let's ride," Barry said . . .

They did not stop to camp until dusk.

O'Brien built the fire.

Kane picketed the horses.

Davis fetched some water.

Hastings stood off to one side with Barry.

"Think we got a posse on our trail?" Hastings asked.

"Why would we?" Barry asked. "Ain't like we robbed their bank."

"No," Hastings said, "but we killed a bartender, and their sheriff."

"We'll set up a watch, then," Barry said. "Just in case."

Hastings asked the other question that had been on his mind.

"How much money did we get?"

"Not enough," Barry said tightly.

"We did get some, though, right?"

"Yeah," Barry said, "but not enough to make it worth the risk."

"How much?"

Barry looked unhappy. He took the money from his pockets, and inside his shirt.

"Those hundred-dollar bills?" Hastings asked with interest.

"Some," Barry said, "but like I said, not enough."

"But how much, Tom?" Hastings asked.

"Okay," Barry said, "this is between you and me. Don't tell the others."

"I ain't gonna tell them nothin'."

"There's four thousand here."

"Four thous—" Hastings started, then lowered his voice. "Four thousand? That's a lot of money."

"Split two ways it's a lot of money," Barry said. "Not split five ways."

"How you gonna keep it from them?" Hastings asked.

"Well," Barry said, "so far you're the only one to ask, but I'll figure somethin' out. Meanwhile, just keep quiet. We'll camp here and get movin' at dawn, just in case there is a posse."

"Okay," Hastings said. Davis was returning with the water, so they fell quiet at that point.

* * *

"He what?" Clint asked.

As they entered the office, the mayor poured two whiskeys and invited Clint to sit. Then he gave him the news.

"Rick has you listed as co-owner of Rick's Place," Jackson said. "So in his absence, you're in charge."

"I can't stay around here and run the saloon," Clint said. "I have to track down the men who shot him."

"Then you'll have to find someone else to run it while he's laid up, and while you're gone."

Clint sipped his whiskey.

"Who would that be?"

"Well, I would've said Henry the bartender, but he's dead, so . . ."

"I have to ride out tomorrow," Clint said, "or they'll have much too much of a head start. How am I going to find someone before then?"

Jackson shrugged, then said, "You have another option, you know."

"What's that?"

"Well, I hesitate to say this, but you could close the place down."

Clint considered that for a moment.

"I could do that," he said then. "That'd be better than turning it over to someone who'd run it into the ground."

"Of course," Jackson said, "closing it will put a lot of people out of work."

Clint frowned. Rick would never do that to his people.

"I'll have to think about it."

"You do that."

"Are you sure about this?" Clint asked. "How do you know Rick's business? That I'm listed as an owner?"

"I'm not only the mayor," Jackson said, "I'm a lawyer—Rick's lawyer."

"Oh, I see."

"Maybe you better follow the doctor's suggestion," Jackson said. "Get something to eat, and then get some rest."

"Yeah," Clint said, "maybe I better." He finished the whiskey and set the glass down on the edge of the desk. "Thanks for the drink, and the information."

"Sure," Mayor Jackson said. "If there's anything else I can do, just let me know."

Clint nodded, and left the office.

ELEVEN

Clint had a quick meal in a small café, then walked over to Rick's Place. The front door was unlocked. He walked in and saw that there were a few people at the bar, a few more seated. Behind the bar were two of the girls, one of whom was Delia.

Clint approached the bar.

"Clint," she said, "this is Jennifer. Can you tell us what happened?"

"Five men broke in this morning, shot and killed Henry, and shot Rick."

"Oh my God," Jennifer said, her hands going to her mouth. "Is he dead?"

"No, Rick is over at the doc's," he said. "Doc Evans got the bullet out, but he doesn't know yet if Rick will make it."

"With Rick hurt and Henry dead, what do we do?" Delia asked.

"Who's in charge?" Jennifer asked.

"Apparently," he said, "I am. According to Mayor Jackson, that is."

"So what are we going to do?" Delia asked.

"I'm not sure," he said. "I'm going to hit the trail tomorrow to track down the men who hit Rick. That means I can either shut the place down, or leave somebody in charge."

"Who?" Jennifer asked.

"Which are you going to do?" Delia asked.

"I don't know," he said. "Look, we'll just keep it open today if you girls are okay tending bar until I make up my mind."

"The other girls will be in soon," Delia said. "We can handle it."

"I'll be in Rick's office for a while."

He walked to the back and went inside. A file drawer was open, an empty cash box was on the floor, and there was blood on the floor. Other than that, there was no indication that anything had happened in the office that morning.

He picked up the cash box and walked around behind the desk and sat, setting the box down on top. He knew Rick kept a cut-down colt in the top drawer, but when he looked, it was not there. He went through some of the other drawers, but didn't know what he was looking for, so he found nothing. He was just groping.

He sat back in the chair, took off his hat, and rubbed his forehead. What was he supposed to do now? He knew Rick would want to keep the place open for his employees. There had to be another male bartender around.

There was a knock on the door at that point.

"Come in."

Delia opened the door, entered, and closed it.

"The other girls are here," she said. "We're going to divvy up the jobs, and alternate behind the bar."

"Whose idea was that?"

"Mine."

"Is there another male bartender?"

"Henry worked all the time," she said. "There is a relief bartender, but he only worked sometimes."

"Is he any good?"

"Rick hired him, and liked him."

"Can you find him?"

"I'm sure we can."

"Okay," Clint said, "bring him in. Delia, what if I left you in charge?"

"Why me?" she asked.

"You're smart and—don't get insulted—you're a little older than the others. Will that be a problem between you and the other girls?"

"I—I don't think so."

"I can leave it up to you," he said. "Run the place as long as you can after I leave. If it gets to be too much, shut it down."

"I think I can handle it," she said, "with the other girls. Don't worry about it, just do what you have to do."

"Thanks, Delia."

"You're not leaving 'til morning, right?" she asked.

"Right."

"Can I . . . come by your room tonight?" she asked. "I think you'll need company."

"I think so, too," he said. "Thanks."

"I'll go back to work and tell the other girls," she said, and left.

"If any of them want to talk to me, I'm available," he said, thinking somebody might have a complaint about the decision.

"I'll tell them," she said, "but I don't think they'll be a problem."

As she left, he sat back in his friend's chair, then decided he couldn't wait any longer. He wanted to go and check on Rick's condition again.

He left the office and started for the door, but stopped short when he recognized a man who was standing at the bar, holding a beer.

Travis.

His stalker.

TWELVE

Watching from his vantage point, Travis had observed the activity in town. He knew there had been some shooting, and somebody was dead. He saw the man shot down in the street, had seen the glint of light off the tin on his chest. And he had recognized Clint Adams when he came running up to the scene, and then went into the saloon. He'd watched as Rick had been carried to the doctor's office, although he didn't know who he was.

He had broken camp, saddled his horse, and ridden into town. By keeping his ears open, drinking in a couple of smaller saloons, he was able to figure out what had happened.

That was when he decided to go to Rick's Place and have a beer.

"What brings you here?" Clint asked, joining him at the bar.

"Beer," Travis said. "Also heard there was some excitement in town."

"Some, yeah."

"Seems to me I been hearing that you're gonna go out after the men who shot up the town. Five men, right?"

"That's the number we got from a couple of witnesses," Clint said.

"Well," Travis said, "seems to me you'd need some help chasing them down."

"Is that right?"

"I heard the sheriff's dead, and there's no deputies."

"That was the case, yeah," Clint said. He took the badge out of his pocket. "They asked me to carry this."

"Well then," Travis said, "you'll be needin' a deputy, won't you?"

"You volunteering?"

"Anybody else step up?"

"Not so far."

"Then you don't have much to pick from, do you?"

"But why would you want to do it?" Clint asked. "You're not from this town, you don't know the people involved."

"I know you," Travis said.

"No, you don't."

"Okay," Travis said, "from what I've observed, you're gonna go after these men alone, and five-to-one odds, that ain't good for anybody."

"If I take somebody with me," Clint said, "it would have to be somebody I knew I could trust to watch my back. You I don't know."

Travis shrugged.

"Suit yourself," he said. He looked pointedly at the badge in Clint's hand. "You're the law."

Clint put the badge back in his pocket. He looked at Delia, who had been watching and listening with interest.

"Delia," he said, "give the man what he wants from the bar on the house." Then he looked at Travis. "Drink your fill and then go."

"I'm gone," Travis assured him.

Clint looked at Delia again.

"I'm going to go and check on Rick's condition, and then I'll be in the sheriff's office."

"Okay."

Clint left the saloon and headed for the doctor's office.

"He's resting comfortably," the doctor said. "That's about all I can say."

"Is he awake?" Clint asked. "Can I talk to him?"

"Let me check."

Clint waited while the doctor went into the other room. When he came back, he said, "You can talk to him for a minute."

"That's all I'll need," Clint said. "Thanks."

Clint went into the other room and saw his friend lying in a bed. He'd been through this kind of scene more than he liked to remember in the past. Rick looked pale, but his eyes were open and—most important—he was breathing.

"Hey," Rick said.

"Rick," Clint said. "How're you feeling?"

"Rocky," his friend said. "I've been waitin' for you."

"Waiting for me? Why?"

"I don't know how long I'll be awake," Rick said, "or alive. I've got to tell you what I know while I can. You are going after them, right?"

"I am," Clint said. "First thing in the morning."

"Well"—Rick licked his lips to moisten them—"one of them called the other one Tom, and I knew I'd seen him in the saloon about a week ago, maybe ten days."

"This Tom?"

"Yeah," Rick said. "He was the leader, and he'd been in here before. When I heard his first name, I got it. His name's Tom Barry."

"Barry," Clint said. "I don't know that name."

"Well, he's the leader," Rick said. "The others do what he says."

"So they're a gang."

"That's what I figure."

"Why did a gang come to town and hit your place rather than a bank?"

"You—you can ask them that when you see them."

"I will. Anything else I can do?"

"Keep . . . keep the place open."

"I am," Clint said. "Delia and the girls are going to take care of it."

"They're good girls," Rick said, his eyes fluttering, "they'll do fine."

"I think so."

Rick nodded weakly.

"Hey," Clint said, "before you go to sleep, you've got to tell me which one shot you."

No answer.

"Rick?"

Still no answer, and from the way he was breathing, Clint could see that he had fallen asleep.

"Yeah, okay," Clint said. "I'll just make them all pay. All five of them."

THIRTEEN

Clint sat behind the desk in the sheriff's office. It was funny—all he'd had when he rode into town was his horse, and now he had two offices, this one and Rick's in the saloon.

First he went through the wanted posters to see if he could find anything for a man named Tom Barry. Normally, he would have sent Rick a telegram to ask him to find out about Barry, but with Rick laid up, he had only one other source. On his way from the doctor's office to the sheriff's office, he had stopped in the telegraph office and sent a message to his friend Talbot Roper, a private detective working out of Denver. If anyone could get him information on the man, Roper could.

He found nothing in the posters. Next he went to the gun rack to see what the lawman had, but there was nothing there that was better than his own Winchester. He remembered, though, that there was a Greener behind the bar at Rick's Place. If it was still there, he could borrow that and take it with him. Fire a shotgun like that into a group of five men and you would immediately cut down the odds.

He left the sheriff's office. Unable to lock the door behind him, he didn't think anyone would go in and steal anything. At least, he hoped no one would. The gun rack was locked, but the key was in the top drawer of the desk. He'd have to suggest to the mayor that they have someone at least sit in the office during the day.

He went to the saloon to check on that Greener.

The place was busy. It was as if word had gone out that Rick was alive, so people thought it was all right to come back.

There was a man behind the bar with Jennifer. Clint looked around, saw Delia working the room with the two other girls.

He stepped to the bar and Jennifer smiled.

"Hi. How's Rick?" she asked.

"He's holding on," he said.

"Beer?" she asked.

"Sure."

"This is Cable," she said, indicating the young man. "He was Henry's relief bartender. That is, when Henry thought he needed relief."

"Which was hardly ever," Cable said. "Hello, Mr. Adams. I heard you're in charge now."

Clint accepted the beer from Jennifer and said to Cable, "That's right. You think you're ready to hire on as the full-time bartender, son?"

"You bet I am."

"Okay, consider yourself hired."

"Thanks."

Delia came over and said, "How's Rick?"

"Okay, so far. I came back for the shotgun behind the bar. If it's still there."

"Somebody picked it up off the floor after . . . well, after this morning. It's there."

She went around the bar, brought the shotgun out, and handed it to him.

"I'm going to take this with me," he said. "I'll bring it back."

"Hey," she said, "you're in charge. It's yours."

"Right. I'm heading for my hotel now, Delia. Going to get some sleep."

"I'll come by later if I can," she said. "Things are pretty busy here."

"I know. I'll see you later, or tomorrow."

Delia nodded and went back to work. Clint left the saloon.

He was beat by the time he got to his hotel, so he took off his boots, stripped down, and got into bed. In moments he was asleep, with his gun hanging on the bedpost.

FOURTEEN

Clint was awakened by a rustling somewhere close to him. When he opened his eyes, he realized he'd been sleeping for a while longer than he'd first guessed. The only light came from the pale half-moon hanging in the sky, which was just enough to illuminate the familiar figure looming directly above him.

"You're here?" he mumbled.

Delia smiled down at him. Her hair was tousled and hung down around both sides of her face like a soft blond curtain. "Told you I'd pay you a visit," she whispered.

Clint reached up to find she was even closer than he'd originally thought. Instead of standing near him, she was lowering herself directly on top of him. More than that, when his hands found her in the near-darkness, they touched smooth naked skin. He moved his hands up and down to find not one stitch of clothing. When he cupped her bare breasts and ran his thumbs against her nipples, Clint's entire body woke up.

"If I'm dreaming, I'd rather not wake up," he said as the tired fog in his head began to clear.

"Let's see," she whispered. Delia reached between his legs to stroke his growing erection. "Seems like you're awake to me." She lowered her mouth onto his cock. Her lips wrapped around him, and she began to lick his shaft from top to bottom. When she felt his hands on her body, she said, "Oh yes. Definitely awake."

"Get over here," he said while taking hold of her and pulling her back on top of him. Rather than climbing onto him, Delia swung a leg over his head and straddled Clint's face. Her slick pussy was directly over his mouth and she moaned softly when he started to lick her. Soon, she lowered her head again and sucked him with renewed vigor.

They tasted each other for a few minutes, Clint licking the moist lips between her thighs while she took his pole into her mouth. It wasn't long, however, before she craved more and crawled forward to sit on his rigid penis. Clint lay back and admired the view as he slipped inside her. Delia's back had a smooth line that started between her shoulder blades and ran all the way down to the slope of her buttocks. Keeping her back to him, she started rocking back and forth while holding on to his legs for support.

Although he enjoyed that well enough, Clint wanted to see her face as he pumped into her. Once again, all he needed to use was his hands to guide her to the exact spot he wanted her to go. Delia was more than willing to oblige him, and with a little bit of repositioning, she was astride him so they could look directly into each other's eyes. Her hair looked like strands of silk in the moonlight, and her skin was cool to the touch. As Clint moved his hands along the front of her body, she closed her eyes and slowly writhed on top of him.

His hands went to her breasts and stayed there as she reached down to guide his cock into her. After taking him all the way inside, she placed her hands on top of his and leaned her head back while letting out a measured breath. Delia ground her hips in a circular motion until he hit just the right spot inside her. Then it was her turn to guide Clint to where she wanted him to go. She moved one of his hands down along her stomach and below her waist. Taking her direction one step further, Clint started rubbing the sensitive nub of flesh just above her opening. Delia gasped as he stroked her clit and soon she was sitting fully upright and massaging her breasts as if she was pleasuring herself in a quiet moment alone.

He kept rubbing her, savoring every moment of the show she was giving him. It wasn't long before she urgently whispered, "Right there. Don't stop. Don't stop."

Clint wouldn't have stopped if two fires had started within a stone's throw of where he was lying. When she climaxed, Delia riding his cock as if she ached to feel every inch of him was almost enough to drive him over the edge. Locking her eyes on to him, she pressed her hands flat against his chest and bucked her hips in a steady pumping motion.

As her pleasure built even more, Delia whipped her hair back and clenched her eyes shut. Sensing she was running out of steam, Clint started thrusting up into her. Although she opened her mouth to speak, she was unable to make a sound. Her legs tightened their grip on either side of him. Her nails dug into his skin. Clint buried his cock between her legs with one last push as Delia's climax finally subsided. Although she was able to open her eyes again and relax somewhat, she was far from through.

Her entire body moved in an almost serpentine rhythm as her hips thrust back and forth. Knowing all too well the effect she was having on him, she rode Clint a little faster. Delia ran a finger between her breasts and then placed that finger upon his lips so he could taste the sweat she'd worked up while riding him. Clint pulled her down to kiss her hungrily as he exploded inside her.

She lay on top of him for a while, running her hand over his chest and slowly shifting her weight. He knew it wouldn't be long before he'd be ready for her again. Judging by the smile on her face, Delia knew it, too.

FIFTEEN

Somebody coughing and spitting woke Tom Barry the next morning. He rolled out of his bedroll, staggered to his feet, and made his way to the campfire.

Irish O'Brien had taken the last watch, so it was he who had put the coffee on. The strong smell of the trail brew popped Barry's eyes open.

"Pour me a cup," he growled at O'Brien.

"Sure, boss."

O'Brien poured it and handed Barry a cup.

"Hey, boss," the Irishman said, "can we talk before the others wake up?"

"Sure, go ahead," Barry said with his nose in his cup. If for no other reason, he'd keep O'Brien around for his coffee.

"The money," O'Brien said, "how'd we do?"

Barry looked at O'Brien. So far he was only the second one to ask about the money.

"Not as well as I thought we'd do," he said.

"Well, I mean, how much is that?"

"About four thousand."

"Four thousand?" O'Brien repeated.

"Shhh," Barry said. "Quiet."

The Irishman lowered his voice.

"That's a lot of money."

"If you're splittin' it two ways, yeah," Barry said, "but not if you're splittin' it five ways."

"I get ya," O'Brien said. He leaned in and lowered his voice even more. "How many ways are we gonna split it?"

"Well . . . if you don't tell anybody about it," Barry said, "it could be two ways."

"I get it," O'Brien said. "You can count on me."

"Good," Barry said, "I knew I could. How about some more of that coffee?"

"Sure, boss," O'Brien said. "You want breakfast?"

"No," he said, "we're gonna get an early start."

"You think there's a posse after us?"

"I don't know," he said, "but we're not gonna take any chances."

"I getcha."

Behind them they heard the other men beginning to stir. Barry was pretty sure Hastings and O'Brien would keep quiet about their conversations. It remained to be seen if the other men would even ask. So far, though, he still had all the money in his possession.

And that was the way he wanted to keep it.

Clint woke early, washed, and dressed without waking Delia. They each knew what they had to do. They had discussed it during the night, so there was no need to go through it again.

He left the hotel, carrying his saddlebags, rifle, and the Greener. He intended to travel light and fast, so all he'd need was his canteen and some beef jerky. He'd pick up his clean laundry the next time he came into town.

He stopped at the doctor's office first.

"He slept through the night," Doc Evans said, "and seems a bit stronger this morning. I'm hopeful."

"Can I see him?"

"He's asleep again," Evans said. "That's the best thing for him."

"Okay, thanks."

"Are you going after them?" Evans asked.

"Right now."

"Alone?"

"I don't have time to get up a posse," Clint said. "Can you think of anybody who would go with me?"

"Truthfully, no," he said. "All we have here are store-keepers and clerks, Mr. Adams. I don't think you could get up a posse even if the bank had been robbed."

"Then I guess I'm on my own," Clint said.

"I'd go with you, but—"

"You've got your job to do here, Doc," Clint said. "Just pull him through."

"I'll do my best."

Clint headed for the door and said, "That makes two of us."

SIXTEEN

Clint picked up the trail outside of town. He'd checked out the ground in front of the saloon, and although the five horses' tracks were in among many others, he'd noticed a couple of things that might help him.

Just outside of town he found a cluster of tracks and got down on one knee to examine them. Sure enough, he found a horse with only three shoes. He didn't know the reason—maybe it had just thrown the fourth one—but this track had also been in front of the saloon. It could have belonged to a customer, but since it was in with the others, he chose to believe that it belonged to one of the robbers.

Satisfied that he had a trail to follow, he mounted up and headed out.

Travis watched as Clint Adams studied the ground. He knew Adams was a competent tracker, but was sure that he was much better. If the Gunsmith had accepted his offer of help, they'd be on their way already.

Adams remained on one knee for some time, then stood up, mounted up, and rode off, going north.

Travis rode down to where Adams had dismounted and took a look for himself, also dismounting. Immediately, he spotted the horse with three shoes. He, too, had seen that track in front of Rick's Place. Could have belonged to a customer, but like Clint, he chose to believe otherwise.

He mounted up and rode after Clint.

Clint rode ten miles and stopped. Here he found the tracks of both horses and men. They had not camped here, but they had stopped, probably to get their breath, or split the money, or simply discuss their options.

If Barry and his men knew enough to know that Rick kept money on hand, they knew enough about the town to figure out that there was no posse after them. That is, unless he was giving them more credit than they deserved.

The tracks of the three-shoed horse confirmed that, so far, he was on the right trail.

He walked around a bit then, satisfied that the tracks had told him all they were going to, mounted up, and headed off again.

Travis once again was not actually following Clint so much as he was trailing him. He also came to the cluster of tracks that showed that the gang had stopped to rest. So far Adams was doing okay in tracking this gang, but the time would come when the tracks dried up. Then what would he do?

Travis mounted up and continued on at a leisurely pace. There was no reason to rush.

Clint made camp, secure in the thought that he was on the right track. As much as he would have liked to continue, there was no point in risking Eclipse's safety, as well as his own, riding in the dark.

He built a fire, made some coffee. He always had some in his saddlebags, even when he was traveling light. He broke off a piece of beef jerky to have for his supper when the coffee was ready.

"I've got beans," Travis said from the darkness.

"You've been out there long enough," Clint said.

"I got a frying pan. You got plates?"

"Come on in."

Travis came into the firelight, leading his horse.

"Hold on," Clint said.

The young man stopped.

"If I let you stay, you going to take off on me again in the morning?"

"I guess that depends on whether or not you accept my second offer of help," Travis said.

"All right," Clint said, "give me the beans and take care of your horse. We'll talk about it over supper."

Travis tossed Clint the pan and beans, and he poured them into the frying pan while Travis saw to his horse. Of course, they'd done this once before, but maybe this time it would end differently.

Travis came over and Clint handed him a cup of coffee.

"Whoee," Travis said after sipping it.

"It's good coffee," Clint said.

"Good and strong."

"Same thing. Beans are ready."

He scooped them onto the plates, handed one to Travis with one of the two forks he always carried. Very often a fork came in much handier than a frying pan. He had broken up the beef jerky and heated it up with the beans.

"It looks to me like you're on the right trail," Travis said.

"Thanks for the confirmation."

"What are you gonna do when the trail runs out?" Travis asked.

"Deal with that when the time comes."

"I can help with that."

"Again," Clint said, "why do you want to help me?"

"I have an interest in you."

"Yeah, and we still haven't gotten to the bottom of that, have we?"

"We can deal with that later," Travis said. "Why don't you just let me help you track these men down?"

"If I do that, I have to know that you can watch my back," Clint said.

"I can do that."

"Tomorrow morning," Clint said, "show me what you can do with a gun. Then we'll talk."

"You want me to target shoot?"

"For a start," Clint said. "For now we better just finished eating and get some sleep. I want to get an early start."

"Want to set a watch?"

"Why?" Clint asked. "Nobody's hunting us. Just get some sleep."

"I'll do the dishes," Travis said.

"Sure," Clint said. "Right now, that's about all I know you can do."

SEVENTEEN

In the morning they had coffee and jerky and got the horses ready.

"You wanted me to shoot some targets, didn't you?" Travis asked.

"Yeah," Clint said, "pick something out."

Travis looked off into the distance.

"Moving or stationary?"

"Stationary, to start."

"How about that branch?"

Clint squinted.

"Where?"

"That cottonwood."

"That's a hundred feet."

"Yeah," Travis said, "but I'm just using my hand gun, right?"

"Okay."

Travis drew and fired without hesitation. The branch flew off the tree.

"Not bad."

"And now it's your turn," Travis said, holstering his gun firmly.

"I've got nothing to prove," Clint said, "and replace that spent round before you holster your gun. That kind of carelessness can get you killed."

Travis looked chagrined, but also angry—probably with himself. He drew the gun, ejected the spent shell, replaced it, and holstered it again.

"Satisfied?" he asked.

"I am for now," Clint said. "Let's start moving. But the time may come when you'll have to prove yourself again."

"And I suppose you never have to prove yourself?" Travis asked.

"No," Clint said. "You already know who I am."

"And why not?"

Clint looked at him.

"Because you already know who I am," he said, "don't you, Travis?"

They mounted up, located the trail again, and started to follow it.

Tom Barry led his gang into the small town of Bronson, in the lower portion of North Texas. It would take them days to get as far as Fort Worth. From there they could hop a train to anywhere, if necessary.

He reined his horse in and stopped before actually entering the town.

"Davis!"

"Yeah?"

"Ride back a ways, make sure there's no posse chasin' us," Barry said.

"Aw, hell," Davis said, "I was lookin' forward to gettin' my ashes hauled."

"Your ashes will have to wait," Barry said. "Ride back about ten miles. If you don't see anybody, come back and get your ashes hauled."

"Okay," Davis said. "I'll see you guys later."

He turned his horse and rode back the way they had come. Barry started his horse forward and led his other men into Bronson.

"How long are we gonna stay here?" Hastings asked.

"Not long."

"Long enough for a meal and a whore?" Irish O'Brien asked him.

"Yeah," Barry said, "that long."

"Long enough for Davis to catch up?" Kane asked.

Barry looked at Kane, then looked away and said, "Yeah, maybe."

EIGHTEEN

Clint and Travis followed the gang's tracks to a town called Bronson.

"They keep goin' in this direction, they'll get to Fort Worth," Travis said.

"I know," Clint said. "If that happens, they can hop a train and be gone in any direction."

When they reached the main street, the tracks got lost among all the others, as well as the ruts in the street caused by wagon traffic.

"We'll have to check the livery stables, hotels, and saloons," Travis commented.

"And the sheriff's office."

Travis looked at Clint.

"I'll leave that to you. I'll check the liveries and meet you in that saloon there," he said, indicating one that said ELLINGTON'S SALOON above the door.

"Then we can check the hotels after we have a beer," Clint said.

"Sounds good to me."

They split up there, and Clint rode over to the sheriff's office.

The office had seen better days. The door had two bullet holes and a cracked pane of glass in it. The town seemed kind of quiet, so maybe the holes were from the good ol' days. He opened the door and stepped in.

There was a musty smell inside, as if the place hadn't seen a broom or an open window for some time. Sitting behind the scarred desk, which leaned to one side because of a broken leg, was a man who fit the scene. In his fifties, overweight, and sleepy looking, he stared at his visitor, as if hoping Clint had come through the wrong door.

"Help ya?"

"You can if you're the sheriff."

"I'm the sheriff," the man said wearily. "No deputies to speak of. I was just taking a load off my feet for a few minutes. What can I do for you?"

"I'm tracking a gang that hit a saloon in Labyrinth, Texas."

"Labyrinth? Where's that?"

That was another reason Clint liked spending time in Labyrinth. It was pretty much unknown even to Texas folks.

"South of here."

"They hit a saloon, you say?" the lawman asked. "Not the bank?"

"No, a saloon."

"Don't think I'd take a posse out to chase down some fellas who shot up a saloon."

"They killed the bartender, the local sheriff, and wounded the saloon owner, who's a friend of mine."

"Must be a good friend."

"He is."

"Not dead?"

"Not so far."

"Who is he?"

"His name's Rick Hartman."

The sheriff frowned.

"I know that name," he said, rubbing his jaw. "And who're you?"

"My name's Clint Adams."

The lawman sat up straighter.

"I know that name, too," he said. "The Gunsmith, right?"

"That's right."

"Well, I wouldn't wanta be the fella you're trackin'," the sheriff said. "What's his name?"

"Tom Barry," Clint said. "He's riding with four others."

"And you tracked them here?"

Clint nodded.

"Their trail leads right to your main street."

"Hm," the man said, rubbing his jaw again, "can't say I seen five men ride in together."

No wonder, Clint thought. There was no way the man could see the street from where he was sitting, and he had a feeling the lawman didn't often move from there.

"I've got one man with me and we're going to be checking the liveries, hotels, and saloons."

"That won't take long," the man said. "We got one livery, one hotel, and two saloons."

"Well, somebody must have seen them."

"Yeah, but are they gonna say so?"

"I intend to find out."

"Okay, I'll be her—I mean, I'll be around if you need anything. Name's Jeff Faraday."

"Sheriff Faraday," Clint said. "I don't think I'll need any help. I just wanted you to know I'm in town, and I guess you could say I was looking for trouble."

"Whatever happens is between you and this Barry fella," the lawman said. "Just don't shoot any innocent citizens."

"I'll try my best not to," Clint said.

He turned and walked out without another word.

The sheriff leaned back in his chair and took a deep breath, let it out slowly. Last thing he needed was trouble from the likes of the Gunsmith.

NINETEEN

Clint met Travis at the saloon. The younger man was already at the bar with a beer. There were about half a dozen others in the place, who looked at Clint curiously when he walked in. He figured it was because he was the second stranger to walk in during the past five or ten minutes.

"Beer," Clint said to the bored-looking bartender.

"Sheriff know anythin'?" Travis asked.

"Not a thing," Clint said, "but I think that's his normal state."

"So he's not gonna be any help."

"Nope. What about here?"

"Didn't ask," he answered. "The liveryman said he hasn't seen five men anytime in the past week. But . . ."

"But what?"

"He seemed real nervous."

"Okay, let's check here first, then we'll go back to the stable."

He turned and waved the bartender over.

"We're looking for five men who may have ridden into town in the past three or four days."

"I don't know nothin'," the man said.

"Does that mean you didn't see them," Clint asked, "or you saw them and you're not talking?"

"It means," the man said, "I ain't sayin' nothin'."

He turned and walked away. Clint studied him for a moment. He was a big man in his thirties, probably used to getting respect because he had thick shoulders and big hands. Clint wasn't impressed, but he also wasn't foolish enough to try to match strength with the man. He thought he could take him, but he didn't want to spend the time, or risk the damage.

He looked at Travis, who raised his eyebrows and then called out, "Hey, bartender."

The big bartender turned and looked at Clint, clearly annoyed, then came back.

"Are you gonna give me trouble, friend?" the barman demanded.

Clint drew his gun and stuck the barrel underneath the man's chin.

"I'm going to give you a lot of trouble," he said.

Clint heard chairs scrape the floor behind him, then heard Travis say, "Stand easy, gents. We're just lookin' for the answers to some questions, that's all."

Clint was depending on Travis to keep the others at bay long enough for him to get those answers.

Travis said to the bartender, "If I was you, I'd answer my friend's question. They're still scraping the last bartender's brains off the ceiling."

"Now," Clint said, "five men would have ridden in here

together in the past three or four days. Chances are they would have been looking for a drink. Think hard."

"Hey, take it easy, mister," the man said. His eyes were wide as he tried to look down at the gun. "F-Four men rode in here and had some drinks, and then a fifth one came in looking for them."

"Looking for them?"

"Y-Yeah," the bartender said. "Near as I can figure, they rode out without him. He was really mad! He said they wasn't gonna cheat him outta his cut."

"When was this?"

"T-Two days ago."

"Two?"

"M-Maybe a day and a half."

Clint removed the gun barrel from the man's chin. The indentation of an "0" was left behind.

"Which way did they go?" Clint asked.

"I—I didn't look when they left," the man said, "but I think they went north."

"That what you told the other man?"

"Yessir."

"How far behind them was he?"

"A f-few hours."

"Okay."

Clint holstered his gun, then looked behind him. Several men had risen from their chairs, but Travis's gun was keeping them in place.

"Go ahead," Clint said to Travis. "'I'll watch your back."

Travis began backing toward the batwing doors, but kept his gun out.

"Anybody want to try?" Clint asked. "Go ahead. I'm just mad enough to kill somebody. No?"

None of the men moved for their guns.

"Then sit down!" Clint snapped.

They all sat.

"First man out that door gets shot," Clint said. "Don't anybody move until you hear us ride out. Got it?"

"W-We got it, mister," the bartender said.

Travis was at the door and said, "Okay."

Clint turned his back on the men and walked to the door, where Travis stood holding one wing open, his gun still in his hand.

Outside the saloon Travis holstered his gun.

"What now?" he asked.

"You did good in there," Clint said.

"You think the bartender told the truth?"

"It's not unusual for thieves to fall out," Clint said. "Yeah, I think he told the truth. Looks like Tom Barry is starting to get rid of his men so he doesn't have to split with them."

"You don't think his other men see what he's doin'?" Travis asked.

"All they see is a bigger cut for themselves," Clint said. "They're not looking beyond that."

"So I guess we're not gettin' a hot meal here, huh?" Travis asked.

"No," Clint said. "We'll stop at the mercantile for a few things and continue north. Maybe we'll catch up to the fifth man. He might help us with the rest."

"Unless he catches up to the rest of them first."

"If they have a falling-out that leads to gunplay," Clint said, "that can only help us."

"We should probably get movin' before somebody inside gets brave," Travis said.

"Good point," Clint said.

As they mounted up, he thought he'd at least found out something he'd been wondering about. Travis could, indeed, watch his back when the time came.

TWENTY

They bought a few supplies, then split them so one man wouldn't have to carry everything.

Outside of town, to the north, they once again picked up the trail of the three-shoed horse.

"Looks to me like it doesn't belong to the fifth man," Travis said.

"Good, so that horse is still with the rest of them," Clint said.

"Could be the following man's horse, the fifth man," Travis said, "but I don't think so."

Clint was mounted, while Travis was down on one knee on the ground.

"Okay, I buy it," Clint said. "Let's move."

Travis mounted up and they started out again.

When they realized they weren't going to catch up to anyone before dark, they decided to camp.

This time they were able to prepare some bacon and

beans, along with Clint's trail coffee. They sat on opposite sides of the fire to eat.

"That's some horse you got there," Travis said. "If you weren't takin' it easy, I doubt mine would be able to keep up with him."

"There's no need to push hard, not yet anyway," Clint said. "When the time comes, you'll just have to do the best you can to keep up."

"Well, my roan ain't so bad," Travis said. "He's got a lot of experience."

"He looks like a decent animal," Clint admitted.

They cleaned up after eating, then Clint made another pot of coffee. They sat and had another cup each.

"Tell me somethin'," Travis said.

"What?"

"Would you have shot that bartender?"

"Just for not talking to me?" Clint asked. "No."

"Not even to help your friend?"

"Killing that bartender in cold blood wouldn't get me to Tom Barry any faster," Clint said. "I'm not a cold-blooded killer. If you've learned anything about me in all this time you've been trailing me, you should have learned that."

"I have," Travis said. "I just wanted to see what you'd say."

"I'll always say what I'm thinking," Clint said. "The truth."

Travis sat quietly and drank his coffee.

In another camp, miles ahead, Zeke Kane asked Barry, "You think Davis is gonna catch up?"

"I told him to make sure we weren't bein' followed,"

Barry said. "I warned him we weren't gonna wait for him, that he'd have to ride hard to catch up." This was a lie.

"He'll make it," O'Brien said to Kane.

"I guess," Kane said.

"We'll set watches for tonight, like usual," Barry said. "Don't anybody shoot poor Davis if he comes ridin' in. Zeke, you're up first."

"Sure, boss."

Kane set his plate down and went to fetch his rifle.

"What do we do if Davis does catch up?" O'Brien asked Barry.

"We'll just tell him we had to keep movin'," Barry said. "He'll buy that. Check on the horses, Irish."

"Right."

That left Barry at the fire with Hastings.

"When do we get rid of them?" Hastings asked.

"As soon as we make sure we're not being followed," Barry said.

"And then we split the money?"

"That's right," Barry lied, "and then we split the money."

TWENTY-ONE

The next day Travis was able to distinguish the tracks of the fifth man.

"He's following them, the way we are," he said. "See? His tracks overlay theirs." He was down on one knee, bent over reading the tracks.

"Okay," Clint said. "How far ahead of us is he?"

"I'd say . . . five hours."

"And the rest of them?"

"A day's ride."

"Okay, then," Clint said, "it may be time to push it."

"Looks like he's pushing it," Travis said. "From the length of the strides, I'd say they're walking, and he's riding hard." He looked back over his shoulder at Clint. "He keeps pushing that horse, he'll ride it into the ground."

"Okay, so we push, but not as hard," Clint said.

Travis stood up, took his reins from Clint, and mounted up.

"I think this old roan can keep up if you don't try to break any speed records."

"Eclipse is built for stamina, not speed."

"Where did you get that horse anyway?" Travis asked.

"It was a gift from a great man," Clint said. He didn't know if Travis would even recognize the name "P. T. Barnum."

"Guess you must've done him a great service."

"We did each other some good," Clint said. "Come on, let's move."

The horse went down, and Cameron Davis went flying over his head. He hit the ground with a bone-jarring thud and lay there a few minutes, trying to catch his breath. By the time he rolled over and stood up to check on his horse, the animal was dead.

"Goddamnit!" he screamed. He threw a couple of punches at the air for good measure, then bent over when the movements caused him some back pain.

Now he'd never catch up to those cheatin' bastards!

He removed his rifle and saddlebags from the fallen horse. He couldn't have gotten the saddle off if he wanted to, wouldn't have been able to carry it if he did. He looked off into the distance and saw a barn. He started walking toward it. Maybe he could get a horse there.

Barry figured if Davis hadn't caught up to them by now, he probably wouldn't. They could afford to stop in the next town, rest the horses, have a meal and a night in a real bed, maybe have a woman, and then move on.

The town was Waco. Big enough to have everything they needed.

Hastings came riding up alongside him.

"The boys wanna know if we're gonna stop," he said.

"Tell 'em yeah, we'll stop overnight. They can do what they want."

"Suits me," Hastings said. "I just want a beer and a steak."

"You got it," Barry said.

As Hastings rode back to tell the other men, Barry put his hand on the saddlebag that had the four thousand in it. Waco might be the place he could get away from the others. He'd have to wait and see if the chance came up.

"We closin' the gap," Travis said, mounting up again. "His horse is shortening stride. It's gonna go down anytime now."

"So unless he finds another one, we'll catch up to him before he catches up to the rest of the gang."

They were riding along and Travis suddenly stood in his stirrups and said, "Maybe sooner than you think."

"Wha—"

"Up there, see it?" Travis said, pointing.

Clint looked into the distance, saw what he thought was a rock, then realized it wasn't.

It was a horse.

TWENTY-TWO

They dismounted when they reached the horse and checked it.

"Dead," Travis said. "Ridden down."

"No saddlebags or rifle," Clint said.

They looked around, saw the barn in the distance. Travis then pointed to the boot prints.

"He headed for that barn."

"If he wants another horse," Clint said, "he's not about to buy it."

"No, he isn't."

"We better get over there."

They mounted up and rode hard for the barn.

Even before they reached the barn and reined in, they heard the shouting.

"You no-good sonofabitch! You can't steal my horse."

It was a woman.

"Inside the barn," Clint said. He dismounted and ran for the door. Travis ran behind him.

As Clint entered, he saw a man holding a saddle in one hand, and a woman in the other. He pushed the woman so that she fell on her ass, and then turned to the horse he was trying to saddle.

"You bastard!" she yelled. "I'll kill you."

As she started to get up, Clint rushed past her, grabbed the man by the shoulder, and spun him around. The man obviously thought it was the woman, but when he saw Clint, his eyes went wide. Clint hit him in the face with one punch and the man went down.

Clint turned to the woman, reached down to help her up. Even under those circumstances he couldn't help noticing how lovely she was. In her forties, she was dressed in a man's shirt and jeans, which did nothing to hide how shapely she was.

She smoothed her long, auburn hair—which was in a wild tangle—and said, "Thanks. He just walked in and started to steal one of my horses."

"You don't have to worry now," Clint said.

"We've been trackin' him, ma'am," Travis said. "He won't bother you anymore."

"What'd he do?"

"Robbed a saloon, shot a friend of mine," Clint said.

"You gonna take him in?"

"Right after he helps us catch the rest of the gang."

"Well," she said, slapping her firm ass to get the dust off it, "you fellas did me a favor, least I can do is return it. It's gettin' late. You're welcome to stay for supper, and then you can bed down in the barn."

Travis looked at Clint, who nodded, and said to the woman, "Much obliged, ma'am. My name's Clint . . . and this is Travis." He decided not to give his last name.

"My name's Laura Wells," she said. "Come on inside. I can give you some coffee now and then cook up some supper."

Clint looked at Travis.

"You go ahead," Travis said. "I'll tie this jasper up and see what he can tell us."

"Okay," Clint said. "See you inside."

He followed Laura to the house, watching the way her behind fit her jeans as she walked.

Travis came in while Clint was drinking coffee. He'd already discovered that Laura lived there alone and raised horses.

"Don't have so many now," she said, "which is why I can't afford to have any stolen."

"Don't blame you," Clint said.

Travis sat down and Laura poured a cup of coffee for him.

"Hope you fellas don't mind stew," she said, stirring a big pot.

"It smells great, ma'am," Travis said. "And I appreciate this coffee. I've been drinking Clint's trail swill for too long."

"My trail swill is just fine," Clint said. "But this *is* better."

Travis sat across from Clint.

"What did you get from him?" Clint asked.

"He's steamin' mad that his friends left without him when they were in Bronson. He figures they're headed for Waco, and then Fort Worth."

"We'll have to take him with us when we leave," Clint said. "We can't leave him here."

Travis looked at Laura.

"Is there a lawman near here?"

"There's a sheriff about ten miles west of here, town called Millard. He'd take him."

Travis looked at Clint.

"That's a ten-mile detour," Clint said.

"We know where they're going," Travis pointed out. "If we get an early start tomorrow . . ."

"We'll have to think about it overnight," Clint said.

"Chow's on, boys," Laura said, carrying two bowls to the table, then fetching one for herself.

They stopped talking and started eating.

TWENTY-THREE

The stew went down smooth, even though the meat was kind of tough. They each had a second bowl, washed down with some more coffee.

"Got some left," she said. "Should I take it out to him?"

"That's right nice of you, wantin' to feed somebody who tried to steal from you," Travis said.

"Don't want it to go to waste," she said "and you don't want him collapsin' from hunger on you."

"No, we don't," Clint said. "Travis, why don't you go get him and bring him in here. Let him eat. Maybe if we show him a kindness, he might have more to say."

"What about the horses?"

"I'll go out and take care of them."

"I'll show you where to put them," Laura said.

"Okay," Clint said. "Thanks."

The three of them went to the barn. Clint and Laura waited outside while Travis untied Davis and then walked him into the house.

That left the two of them alone.

"You mind if I ask you somethin'?" she asked.

"Sure, go ahead."

"You like the way I look?"

"Wha—well, yeah, I think you're beautiful."

"Been a long time since I been with a man," she said, "and I find you right appealing."

"Well . . . I'm flattered."

"Won't take long," she said. "we can just go right there in the barn."

"Laura," he said, "you're obviously not a woman a man wants to rush with."

She smiled at him and asked, "Is that sweet talk?"

"I guess it is."

Laura took Clint by the hand and led him into the drafty old barn. "I couldn't wait another second," she said.

Clint allowed his eyes to linger on the rounded curves of her breasts and the smooth, creamy skin of cleavage displayed by her tight-fitting clothes. She had managed to already undo the top two buttons of her shirt. "I've been thinking of a few things myself," he told her.

"Like what?"

He answered by moving closer to her and taking her in his arms. She responded without a struggle and kissed him deeply. Her lips parted so she could slip her tongue into his mouth, and her hand wandered between his legs to feel the growing bulge in his crotch. As she massaged him, she kissed him harder. He was surprised when she suddenly pulled away from him, but was encouraged by the mischievous smile she wore.

Tugging at his belt, Laura unbuckled it so she could

loosen his pants and pull them down while lowering herself to her knees in front of him. He set his gun down on the ground right next to them. His cock was already hard and it became even harder as she slowly moved her mouth toward it. Clint could feel her hot breath moments before Laura's tongue flicked along the tip of his penis. "That's the way," he said while sliding his fingers through her hair. "Just like that."

Laura reached around to hold his hips with both hands while easing him all the way into her mouth. Once her lips closed around the base of his shaft, she began sucking on him noisily. Her head bobbed back and forth as her tongue slid over every inch of his thick member as though she were savoring a stick of candy. Then, she swirled her tongue around the head of his cock until he felt his toes curling inside his boots. It wouldn't be long before she pushed him over the edge, so Clint moved her head away and took a step back.

"What's the matter?" she asked with a pout. "Didn't you like that?"

He helped her to her feet and said, "You know damn well I liked it." There was a bale of hay nearby. He took her there and spun her around so her back was facing him. Then he anxiously peeled back the layers of material separating him from what he was after. Once all of Laura's garments were removed, he could see the rounded curve of her ass, which led up to the gentle slope at the small of her back. He ran his hands up and down those curves until she began to moan softly like a cat purring in contentment. She placed her hands flat upon the hay bale, and looked back at him over her shoulder.

"Don't make me wait for it," she said.

Never one to refuse a lady, Clint positioned himself behind her and guided his cock between her thighs. Her warm pussy was dripping wet, and Laura moved her legs apart to allow him to slip inside with ease. When Clint grabbed her hips with both hands, Laura tossed her hair back and grunted while taking every inch of him inside.

He kept one hand on her hip while placing the other at the small of her back. That way, he could feel every one of her movements as she responded to him. When he pumped into her, Laura's muscles tensed. When he eased back out again, she let out a breath and rocked back as if desperate for him to fill her once more. Soon, he found himself pounding into her harder.

"Yes," she groaned. "God, yes."

When he buried his cock all the way into her, Clint reached forward to grab a handful of Laura's hair. She dug her fingers deep into the hay bale as he gave her hair a tug and thrust into her again. Soon, Clint could feel her pussy gripping him tighter and her entire body start to tremble. He gave her rump a smack that was just loud enough to be heard before he drove into her again. Laura cried out as she climaxed, but Clint didn't ease up.

First, he placed his hands on her shoulders while continuing to pump into her from behind. Laura was breathless and moaning softly for him to keep fucking her. Then, Clint cupped her breasts with both hands as they swayed in time to his movements. He rubbed her plump tits and teased her nipples, which was enough to drive her to new heights. Finally, he moved his hands back to her hips so he could finish what he'd started.

The sensations continued to build in Clint's body and the heat inside him grew to a blaze when he looked down to see Laura's rounded ass in his hands. She grunted and groaned like an animal, which was music to his ears. Soon, the pressure inside him reached its peak and Clint impaled her one last time.

He straightened up and let out a slow breath as he emptied into her. When he loosened his grip on her, she moved forward until he slipped out of her so she could turn around to face him.

TWENTY-FOUR

They got dressed and she showed him what stalls to put their horses in. She helped him by unsaddling and brushing down Travis's horse, and they put feed out for both of them.

"How do I look?" she asked.

"Great."

"Out of breath."

"Maybe," he said, "but that would make two of us."

"Think Travis will know what we been up to?"

"Maybe not," he said, "and speaking of Travis . . . why me, and not him? He's younger, better looking—"

"I went for experience," she said. "I don't think I made the wrong decision, do you?"

"Definitely not."

She smiled. They left the barn together and walked back to the house.

As they entered the kitchen, Travis said, "I was just about to bring him back out there."

"He's done already?" she asked.

"Wolfed it down," Travis said.

"Okay, then, better take him back out there and tie him up good."

"I'll stay out there, too," Travis said. "I'm ready to bed down, and we want to get an early start."

"Whataya gonna do with me?" Davis demanded.

"We don't know yet," Clint said. "Just be grateful we fed you."

"Well, I didn't do noth—"

"Shut up!" Travis said, swatting the back of Davis's head.

"I'll be right out," Clint said. "One last cup of coffee."

"Sure." Travis turned to the outlaw, pulled him up from his seat by the back of his shirt. "Come on, you."

He pushed him out the door ahead of him.

Laura covered her mouth and looked at Clint.

"What?" he asked.

"You think he knows? And he thinks he's leavin' us alone so we can . . . you know."

"Well, we already . . . you know . . . I do need to get an early start tomorrow. And I'm tired, for some reason."

"Maybe," she said with a mischievous smile, "I should have picked the younger man."

"Just give me another cup of coffee, woman," Clint growled at her.

Clint walked back to the barn after his last cup of coffee and found that Travis had set himself up across the building from Davis, who was tied up and snoring.

"I see you got him bedded down all right," Clint said.

"Yeah, although I don't know how he can sleep so soundly all trussed up like that."

"It's the sleep of the guilty," Clint said.

"Huh?"

"A guilty man sleeps soundly because he knows he's guilty," Clint said. "An innocent man lies awake, worried that he's going to be blamed for something he didn't do."

Travis frowned and said, "I guess that makes sense."

"That's the way it was explained to me anyway."

"Enjoy your last cup of coffee?" Travis asked, changing the subject.

"I did, thanks."

"You sure you want to sleep out here with us peasants?" Travis asked.

Clint grabbed his bedroll and walked to one of the empty stalls.

"Why don't you just go on and sleep in the house?" Clint asked.

"Hey, the lady never looked at me twice," the younger man said.

Clint dropped his bedroll down on the floor of the stall. A few feet away was the bale of hay he and Laura had used. He was surprised it didn't bear the outlines of their bodies.

"So what do we want to do tomorrow?" Travis asked, sounding as if he was stretching at the same time.

"Laura says she'll make us breakfast, and then we can get an early start," Clint said.

"Seems to me you still got time to sneak over to the house—" Travis started.

"Will you go to sleep," Clint snapped.

"Why don't you both shut up and go to sleep so I can sleep?" Davis whined.

"See what you did?" Clint said to Travis. "You woke up the bad man."

Clint heard deep breathing from Travis's direction, couldn't believe that the man had fallen asleep while he was talking to him.

TWENTY-FIVE

In the morning Laura made eggs for them to the best of her abilities. They were a little dry, but hot.

"These eggs are really—" Davis started to complain, but a hard look from Clint changed his mind. "Good."

"If you had just asked me to sell you a horse, I probably would have," Laura said. "And then I might have even cooked you a meal."

Davis was young, just a little older than Travis, and probably did very well with the ladies. Clint wondered what else he would have gotten if he had been the only man there.

"That brings up a problem," Travis said.

"What's that?" Clint asked.

"We need a horse for Davis."

Clint looked at the man and said, "Well, we could make him walk."

"Aw no . . ." Davis said.

"I can lend you a horse," Laura said. "You can leave it for me at the livery in Millard."

Clint and Travis exchanged a glance.

"I guess that means we're goin' to Millard," Travis said.

"Or," Clint said, "one of us could go to Millard and the other could stay on the trail."

"And which one of us do you have staying on the trail?" Travis asked.

"Well, me, of course," Clint said.

"And so you'll catch up to them and have nobody to watch your back."

"You'll catch up to me before then," Clint said.

"Maybe."

"All right, then," Clint said, "we'll both go to Millard. It's not that big a detour."

"I could take him to Millard," Laura said.

They both looked at her.

Sure," she said. "Tie him up and throw him in the back of my buckboard. I'll take him to the sheriff and tell him what happened."

"Do you have a gun?" Travis asked.

"A rifle," she said. "I was out in the barn when he got here, and my rifle was in the house, or I would've run him off. Believe me, I can take care of myself."

Again, Clint and Travis exchanged a glance.

"Hey, the lady can take me," Davis said. "I won't try nothin'."

"If you do," she said, "it's the last thing you'll ever try."

"What do you think?" Travis asked.

"Oh, come on," she said. "I have to go to town for supplies anyway. What harm can he do tied up?"

"We wouldn't lose any time this way," Clint said.

"But I'll do it under one condition."

"What's that?" Clint asked.

"That you stop here on your way back and tell me what happened."

"It's a deal," Clint said.

"Then we better all get ready to go," Travis said.

About twenty minutes later Clint and Travis dumped Davis, trussed up even better than he had been overnight, into the back of Laura's buckboard. She was sitting in her seat with her rifle propped next to her.

"Now don't stop anywhere along the way," Clint said. "Just get him to town as quickly as you can."

"Don't worry," she said, "I can handle this."

They went to the livery and brought their saddled horses out. They rode part of the way with her, but when the road forked, she headed for Millard, and they headed north.

TWENTY-SIX

Sitting at a table in the Queen of Hearts Saloon in Waco, Tom Barry nursed a beer and tried to figure out how to get rid of his men.

Kane and O'Brien were standing at the bar. Hastings was off someplace with some whore. It occurred to Barry that if he could get Kane and O'Brien killed in a bar fight, he wouldn't have to worry about them anymore. And he could tell Hastings it wasn't his fault.

He looked around him, spotted two tables with poker games going on. Both games had house dealers. At one table the chips were pretty much evenly distributed. The other table, however, presented a different story. One player had most of the chips in front of him. Three of the other players didn't seem to mind that much, as if their attitude was "ho hum, just another night of losing money . . ."

One man, however, was not as resigned as the others. Barry could see that if he was any madder, he'd have steam coming out of his ears.

This was his man.

Barry watched and listened, saw the man throw his cards down and exclaim, "How the hell—I just can't figure it." He was getting furious.

All Barry had to do was wait . . .

Tracy Hastings stared out the window of the whorehouse. He knew down deep that after Tom Barry managed to get rid of both Kane and Irish O'Brien, he'd get rid of him, too. And for only four thousand dollars. The best thing for him to do would be to ride out now and forget about it. Only he couldn't. He didn't want to let Barry get the better of him.

"Hey, baby," the whore said from behind him. "You gonna leave me like this?"

He turned and looked at her. She had a wide ass, big pendulous breasts, was forty if she was a day, but it had been a while since he'd been with a woman. She had nice skin, and she smelled good. He'd been right in the middle of fucking her when he started to think. When he started to think, his dick got soft.

"Come on, baby," she said, "I'll get it hard for you again. I know just how to do it."

"I bet you do," Hastings said.

"Don't make me come over there and grab you by your tallywacker," she said. "Bring it over here and I'll suck it dry."

He felt it twitch. He loved it when a whore talked dirty to him.

"Whatever you're thinkin' about," she said, "why don't you think about it later."

"Okay," he said, turning to face her, "you got me convinced."

* * *

"Where's Hastings?" Kane asked.

"He's at the whorehouse."

"Why ain't we at the whorehouse?" Kane asked.

"Because we wanted whiskey first."

"What the hell is wrong with us?"

"Damned if I know."

"How long we stayin' here?" Kane asked.

"Barry said overnight."

"Then we better go get fucked," Kane said.

"I agree."

They drained their glasses and slapped them down on the bar.

Sometimes, Tom Barry thought, things just work in your favor. As soon as Kane and O'Brien left the saloon, the fella at the poker table won a few hands.

It was perfect.

Clint and Travis camped about thirty miles outside Waco.

"If we rode all night, we could make it," Travis said.

"I want them bad," Clint said, "but not bad enough to risk my neck, and my horse, at night. Why don't you go ahead and I'll meet you there."

"Because I'm here to cover your back," Travis said. "I can't do that if I ride ahead of you, can I?"

"Then shut up and drink the coffee and eat the beans," Clint said.

"I'll eat the beans," Travis said, "but I'm not going to drink any more of your coffee. I think I'll just drink water out of my canteen."

"Suit yourself," Clint said, picking up the pot. "More for me."

"How the hell have your insides not just rotted away?" Travis asked.

"They probably have," Clint said. "They probably already have."

TWENTY-SEVEN

The poker player took the break Barry was waiting for. As he got up from the table and walked to the bar, so did Tom Barry.

As the man ordered a drink, Barry sidled up alongside him and said, "I'll have one, too, on my friend here."

The man looked at him and asked, "Why would I buy you a drink? I don't know you."

"You're gonna buy me a drink because I've got somethin' to tell you. Somethin' you're gonna find real interestin'."

"Is that a fact?"

"It is."

The man studied him for a moment, then looked at the bartender. "Steve, get the man a drink."

"My name's Tom Barry," Barry said.

"Drew Stubbs," the gambler said. "What's on your mind?"

Barry took the whiskey from the bartender.

"Seems your luck has changed, all of a sudden."

"So?"

"Ever wonder how that happens?"

"No," Stubbs said. "I play enough to know that it does, though."

"Well," Barry said, "today I can tell you why."

"Is that a fact?"

"It is."

"Okay, then . . . why?"

Barry drained his glass and held it up.

"Give him another, Steve," Stubbs said. "This better be good."

"Oh," Barry said, "it will be."

Stubbs listened to what Barry had to say, then looked at the bartender.

"What about it, Steve?"

"Well, he's right about one thing," the bartender said. "There was two fellas standing right here."

Stubbs turned and looked at the card table. He saw that someone could easily see his cards from here.

"Did they signal anybody?" he asked.

"I wouldn't know," the barman said, "but then if they was sendin' signals, they wouldn't do it so anybody could see, would they?"

"No," Stubbs said, "they wouldn't."

Stubbs looked at Barry, but spoke to the bartender.

"And did my luck change as soon as they left?"

"Seemed to," the bartender said.

"Shit," Stubbs said.

"I told you it'd be interestin'," Barry said.

Stubbs looked at Steve and asked, "Where are the boys?"

"Whorehouse."

"And what were these two fellas talkin' about before they left?"

"Going to the whorehouse," Steve said. "In fact, they asked me where it was."

Stubbs drank his whiskey down and said, "Perfect."

Kane was in a room at the whorehouse with a little blonde, while O'Brien had picked out an Irish-looking girl who said he could call her Sinead. She had long brown hair, long legs, and pert little tits.

Kane had the blonde on her belly, was rubbing his long, skinny dick on her ass cheeks, when the door slammed open.

"What the—" he said, looking over his shoulder. Three men entered the room, guns drawn.

"This is what we do to cheaters in Waco," one of them said.

He grabbed Kane by his long hair and pulled him off the bed, dragging him to the floor.

"What the hell—" he started, but that's as far as he got before they cut his throat.

In a room down the hall, O'Brien didn't hear the ruckus. He was too busy watching the Irish-looking girl. She was undressing in slow motion, first uncovering her hard, brown nipples, and then the big bush between her legs. That done, she ran her hands over her own body, sliding one hand down between her legs.

O'Brien had a raging erection when the door to the room slammed open.

"Hey, what do you think—"

Three men entered, guns in their hands. One of them already had blood on him as he drew a knife.

O'Brien made a grab for his gun, but it was too far away.

"This is what happens to cheaters," the man with the knife said.

O'Brien felt a hand beneath his chin, and then intense pain before . . .

In still another room Tracy Hastings heard the activity, got off the bed, and opened the door to his room only slightly. He saw three men in the hall, one of them covered with blood. He waited until they had gone down the steps before he opened the door and ran down the hall, naked. He looked into the room with the open door, saw a frightened girl on the bed, and Irish O'Brien on the floor with his throat cut.

"What happened?" he asked the girl.

She stared at him and said, "I don't know nothin'!"

He moved farther down the hall, found another open door. Another girl, this one blond, was on the bed with her knees drawn up to her chest, her arms wrapped around them. On the floor Kane lay in a pool of blood, a great, yawning wound where his throat used to be.

"Jesus," he said. He looked at the girl. "What the hell happened in here?"

"T-They just came in and . . . and killed him," she said.

"Who?"

"I—I don't know," she said.

"You didn't recognize them?"

The girl stared at him for a moment, then lifted her chin and said, "I don't know nothin'."

TWENTY-EIGHT

Clint and Travis rode into Waco in the afternoon. Clint had decided to stop first at the sheriff's office. Travis had no objection.

They reined in and tied their horses in front, knocked on the door, and entered.

A man was coming out of the cell block carrying a tray. He stopped and looked at them.

"Feeding time at the zoo," he said. "Lunch."

"Are you the sheriff?" Clint asked.

"I am. Sheriff Mike Dalman." He was gray-haired, solidly built, in his fifties. "What can I do for you?" He put the tray down on his desk, hung the cell keys on a wooden peg. His gun was also hanging there.

"My name's Clint Adams," Clint said. "This is my partner, Travis."

"Adams?" the sheriff said. "The Gunsmith?"

"That's right," Travis said.

"What are you doin' in Waco?"

"We tracked four men here," Clint said.

"Tracked? Are you lawmen? Or bounty hunters?"

"Neither," Clint said. "They shot and robbed a friend of mine in Labyrinth, Texas."

"Labyrinth? Where's that?"

"South Texas."

"He dead?"

"Not when I left."

"If he's dead, it's murder."

"I know that."

"You know the names of the men you're trackin'?" Dalman asked.

Over breakfast Davis had given them the names of the men riding with Tom Barry.

"Tracy Hastings, Irish O'Brien, and Zeke Kane. They're riding with a man named Tom Barry."

"O'Brien and Kane, huh?"

"That's right."

"Well, you won't have to worry about them anymore," Dalman said.

"Why's that?"

"They're dead."

"Who killed 'em?" Travis asked.

The sheriff jerked his thumb back into the cells and said, "The fellas I got locked up in there."

"Why?" Clint asked. "What happened?"

"Well, I've got a fella named Stubbs in there who thinks that O'Brien and Kane were cheating him at cards."

"They were playin' cards?" Travis asked.

"No, they were standin' behind him at the bar, signaling to someone what his cards were. He didn't take kindly to that, so he and two of his compadres cut their throats."

"In the saloon?" Travis asked.

"No, the whorehouse," Dalman said. "I arrested them for murder."

"Why did they think O'Brien and Kane were cheating?" Clint asked.

"Apparently, that's what Stubbs was told."

"By who?"

"A fella named Tom Barry."

"Barry gave up his own men?" Travis asked.

"He's down to one," Clint said. "He's only got Hastings to get rid of and then he can keep the money for himself."

"Typical," the sheriff said. "Thieves fallin' out."

"Can I talk to the prisoners?" Clint asked.

"Sure, I don't see why not," Dalman said. "Go ahead in."

"Thanks."

"Leave your guns with me," Dalman said.

Travis started to take his off, but Clint said, "I can't give up my gun, Sheriff. You understand. I'll stay away from the bars."

Dalman frowned, then said, "Yeah, okay."

Travis took his hands away from his gun belt, and followed Clint into the cell block.

There were three men, each in a cell, all three lying on their cots.

"Hello, gents," Clint said. "I hear you fellas took care of some card cheats."

One man lifted his head to look at him. The others remained as they were, one on his side, the other on his back with his arm across his eyes.

"What's it to you?" the man asked.

"Which one are you?" Clint asked.

"Stubbs."

"Ah, the card player."

"I play, yeah. What of it?"

"I understand how mad a cheater can make you, Drew, but cutting their throats was not the way to go."

Stubbs stuck his prominent chin out and said, "I got mad."

"Or somebody got you mad," Clint said.

Stubbs didn't say anything.

"Seems a fella named Barry got you all riled up," Clint said.

"So?"

"So I'm looking for Tom Barry."

"Well, you better find him before I do," Drew Stubbs growled.

"That looks pretty likely," Clint said. "I'm out here and you're in there."

Stubbs stuck his chin out again.

"When I track him down," Clint said, "I can give him your best."

"Before you do what?"

"Kill him."

Stubbs rubbed his jaw now and said, "That don't sound too bad. Whataya need from me?"

"Anything you can give us," Clint said. "Something he said, maybe."

"He just told me the names of the men who were cheating me," Stubbs said.

"And you believed him?"

"Why not?" Stubbs demanded. "I was losing while they were there, and I started to win after they left. What would you think?"

"That my luck had changed, period. Nobody's fault," Clint said. "But hey, that's just me. Did he tell you who they were passing signals to?" Clint asked.

Stubbs looked uncomfortable with that question.

"Um, no, he didn't."

"Because really, that's the person who was cheating you, wasn't it?"

"I suppose."

"So Barry was probably lying to you."

Stubbs frowned.

"You mean . . . they wasn't really cheatin', after all?" he asked.

"No, maybe they weren't."

"So I killed two innocent men?"

"Well, they weren't innocent," Clint said. "In fact, there might even be a reward—but you'd have to get out jail to collect it."

"Can you get me out?" he asked, tightening his hands on the bars.

"Hey," one of the other men said, "us, too."

"Sorry," Clint said, "there's nothing I can do to get any of you out. You're going to have to stand trial. But like I said, I can give Barry your best."

"Even if I can't help you?" Stubbs said. "I don't know nothin'."

"That's okay," Clint said. "I'll do it anyway."

"Then do me a real favor, mister."

"What's that?"

"When you catch up to the sonofabitch," Stubbs said, "give him my worst."

TWENTY-NINE

When they came out of the cell block, the sheriff asked, "Find out anything?" He was seated behind his desk.

"No, nothing," Clint said, "but thanks for letting us talk to them."

"No problem."

"Sheriff, did you have any dealings with Tom Barry, or the other man?"

"No, by the time Stubbs told me who sent him after the two dead men, your man Barry was gone, and the other fella with him."

"I see."

"Sorry you didn't learn more," Dalman said.

"That's okay," Clint said. "Thanks."

"You leavin' town now?"

"Right now," Clint said. "You won't get any trouble from me."

"Appreciate that," the sheriff said.

They stepped outside and Travis asked, "You believe 'im?"

"Who? Stubbs, or the sheriff?"

"Both."

"Yeah, I believe them," Clint said. "Barry just found himself a hothead to take care of his problem for him."

"And the sheriff?"

"He's got three killers in his jail," Clint said. "I don't see that he has any reason to lie."

"Then we're out of Waco?"

Clint nodded.

"We're out of here."

Tom Barry and Tracy Hastings had left Waco the night before, in the wake of the killings. They had gone a good ten miles in the dark, and then made camp.

Hastings slept with one eye open. He knew Barry had to have something to do with the killing of Kane and O'Brien; he just didn't know what. As far as he knew, Barry was not acquainted with the men who did the killings.

By morning they had switched places, with Hastings on watch. Briefly he considered trying to kill Barry in his sleep, but there was always the chance the other man was also sleeping with one eye open. There was also the chance that Barry might decide to split the money with Hastings and maintain their partnership. After all, they had known each other a lot longer than either of them had known the other men.

But in all that time they'd known each other, Tom Barry had never revealed a soft spot for anyone or anything other than his own pocket.

Hastings smelled the coffee, went over, and nudged Barry with his toe.

"Coffee's ready," he said.

Barry coughed, spat, rolled over, and got to his feet slowly.

"Gimme a cup!" he growled. He hawked and spat again.

Hastings poured a cup of coffee and handed it to him.

"Seems to me," he said to Barry, "it's time to split the money."

"That how it seems to you, Tracy?"

"Yeah."

"Whatsamatta, you don't trust me no more?"

"The question should be, did I ever trust you, Tom?" Hastings said.

Tom Barry lowered the coffee cup and stared at the other man, who did not back down from his gaze, as other men had in the past.

"Tracy," he said, "we gotta stick together. We still don't know if anybody's on our trail. If there is, we're better off watchin' each other's back. Let's just give it a little more time. Whataya say?"

Hastings studied Barry for a moment, then gave in.

"Yeah, okay, Tom," he said. "Just a little longer."

THIRTY

Clint and Travis left Waco, found the point where Tom Barry and Tracy Hastings had camped.

"They didn't get very far," Travis said.

"Seems to me they left at night," Clint said. "They probably just picked their way this far in the darkness and decided to camp rather than risk one of their horses breaking a leg."

"Probably."

Travis held his hand over the dead fire.

"Cold," he said. "They're still half a day ahead, maybe more."

"Heading for Fort Worth."

Travis stood up.

"We should've left sooner."

"We only took time for a meal and a telegram," Clint said. "I needed to find out if Rick was still hanging in there."

And he was. The doctor had replied almost instantly to his telegram that Rick Hartman was still alive.

"Come on," Clint said. "If you're impatient, we should probably start moving a little faster." He mounted up. "Now we'll find out how well your roan can keep up."

By midday Travis's roan was winded from trying to keep up with Clint.

"You want to outrun me? Go ahead, but my horse needs a rest." Travis dismounted.

"No problem," Clint said. "We'll take a short rest." He also dismounted.

Travis walked his roan to a nearby stream, and Clint followed. They allowed the horses to drink while they also drank from their canteens, and refilled them.

"You can go on ahead of me, you know," Travis said. "I mean, if that was what you wanted to do. There's only two of them left. The odds have gotten a lot better."

"Hey," Clint said, "you've come this far with me. Besides, if I did ride on ahead, you'd just keep trailing me, right? Like you've been doing?"

"That's right."

"There you go," Clint said. "So just take a breath, and then we'll be on our way again."

Clint went to work checking the cinch on Eclipse's saddle, and keeping the horse from drinking too much water.

Travis was checking each of his horse's hooves for debris that might injure or hinder the animal. Clint did the same.

"You know," Travis said, "if this takes much longer,

it seems like Tom Barry will take care of all the other men for us. We'll only have him to deal with."

"If we catch him," Clint said. "If he gets to Fort Worth, he could be gone."

"Would you keep searching for him?"

"Yes."

"No matter where you had to go?"

"Yes."

"Why?"

"He shot a friend of mine."

"So you're takin' it personally?"

"You bet," Clint said. "I don't have that many good friends that I can let it go."

"Then we better push on to Fort Worth," Travis said, "and stop tracking him."

"Well," Clint said, "he's going in that direction, but what if he's not actually going there? If we just ride straight there, we might lose him."

"So you believe we should just keep on his trail?" Travis asked.

"Yes," Clint said, "for now. It won't be that much farther. And if he veers off and goes someplace else, we'll know."

Okay, then." Travis mounted his roan, watched while Clint mounted Eclipse. "You know, there's another option."

"What's that?"

"Push the horses, try to ride him down. Instead of following him to Fort Worth, or wherever he's going, catch up to him before he reaches his goal."

Clint gave the suggestion some thought.

"What are you thinkin'?" Travis asked.

"Let's ride," Clint said. "I'll tell you along the way."

* * *

"I've been thinking," Clint said, "about five men hitting a saloon."

"Thinking what?"

"Why do it?"

"For the money."

"If you want money, you hit a bank, not a saloon," Clint said.

"You think there was another reason?"

"Must be."

"And you want to find out what it is."

"Yes."

"So you think somebody sent them after your friend?" Travis asked. "That they were supposed to kill him?"

"That's what I want to find out."

"So that's why we're followin' him and not tryin' to ride him down."

"Right."

"Well, thanks for tellin' me."

"I've been busy convincing myself," Clint said, "so I suppose we'll see when we get where we're all going."

THIRTY-ONE

"You know what I'm still tryin' to figure?" Hastings asked Tom Barry.

"What?"

"Why you decided to hit that saloon."

Barry gave Hastings a momentary glance, then looked straight ahead.

"I told you," he said, "I figured there was some money there."

"More than four thousand, right?"

"A lot more."

Hastings fell silent.

"Why?" Barry asked. "What's your problem?"

Hastings hesitated, then said, "Your research is usually a lot better than that."

"Everybody makes mistakes."

"Not you, Tom," Hastings said, "not unless you want to make a mistake."

"Whataya gettin' at, Tracy?" Barry demanded.

"Nothin'," Hastings said, "I'm just wonderin', that's all."

"Well, stop wonderin'," Barry said. "That's my advice to you."

"Sure, Tom," Hastings said, "whatever you say."

They were ten miles from Fort Worth when Tom Barry suddenly changed direction.

Hastings noticed it, but did not speak until they had gone a few miles.

He reined in.

Barry continued on for a few yards before he stopped and turned.

"What's wrong?"

"Whataya mean, 'what's wrong'?" Hastings asked. "We ain't headed for Fort Worth anymore, Tom, that's what's wrong."

Barry rode back to stand beside Hastings.

"What's goin' on?" Hastings asked.

"You wanna go to Fort Worth, go ahead," Barry said.

"I ain't sayin' that," Hastings responded. "Just give me some idea what we're doin', Tom. Or if you're gonna try to kill me like the others, go ahead. Draw down. Do it now."

Tom Barry stared at Hastings.

"I ain't gonna kill you, Tracy."

"That's good to hear," Hastings said, "but where the hell are we goin'?"

"Just follow me," Barry said. "I'll tell you when we get there. How's that?"

Hastings hesitated.

"Just stick with me."

"Yeah," Hastings said after a moment, "okay. Go ahead, let's go."

"You won't be sorry."

They started off again and rode the rest of the way in silence.

They bypassed a town called Liberty, and Hastings didn't question Barry again. As they approached a ranch, Hastings had an idea of what was happening.

"This is a big spread," he said.

"Yeah, it is."

"Somebody who lives here has a lot of money."

"Yeah, he does."

"So that's it?" Hastings asked. "You got hired to do this?"

"Yeah, I did."

"That's why you never seemed that upset about the four thousand," Hastings said. "You're gettin' paid for this."

"We're gettin' paid for this, Tracy," Barry said. "There's two of us."

"How much?"

"Wait and see, my friend," Barry said. "Wait and see. Come in, the man is waitin'."

THIRTY-TWO

"Here," Travis said.

Clint rode up alongside the younger man and looked down at the ground.

"They changed direction here," Travis said.

"So they're not going to Fort Worth."

"Looks like it."

"What are they up to?" Clint asked, looking off to the east, the direction they were now going.

"What town is that way?" Travis asked.

"Not sure," Clint said. "I guess we'll just have to follow and find out."

"They might be goin' to meet someone," Travis said. "That would support what you've been thinking."

"What I've been toying with," Clint said.

"Your friend Hartman, does he have many enemies?" Travis asked.

"Everybody's got enemies," Clint said, "and he's a businessman, so he probably has more than most."

"Well," Travis said, "could be somebody don't like the way he does business."

"Could be," Clint said.

Travis looked at the ground again.

"They're stayin' together," he said, "so the odds are even."

"Until they get where they're going," Clint said, "then we don't have any idea of the odds."

"But you're gonna let them get there, aren't you?"

"Yes, I am."

"Well," Travis said, "I guess there's no point in pushin' the horses anymore. We know where they *ain't* goin', and I'd say we're only a few hours behind them."

"If we come to a town first," Clint said, "we'll stop and see if they have a telegraph office."

"Suit yourself," Travis said. "You're callin' the play."

"You can still ride on."

Travis shook his head.

"I came this far," he said, "might as well see it through the rest of the way."

"All right," Clint said, "but when this is over, I think I'm going to deserve the answer to a question."

"Really?" Travis asked. "I'm helping you out, and you think you deserve somethin'?"

"I'm letting you ride with me," Clint said.

"To watch your back," Travis reminded him.

"Only I didn't ask for your help."

Travis looked stubborn.

"Okay," Clint said, "I guess we'll have to deal with this later."

"I guess we will."

* * *

As they rode up to the large house, several men in a corral stopped what they were doing to watch them.

"You know them fellas?" Hastings asked.

"Nope."

"But you're expected here, right?"

"That's right," Barry said. "Don't worry, we won't have no trouble here."

"I'm always expecting trouble, Tom," Hastings said. "You know that."

"I do," Barry said. "That's what I like about you, Tracy. You're always ready."

They stopped their horses in front of the house and dismounted.

Barry started up the steps to the front door and Hastings asked, "What about the horses?"

Barry gestured toward the men in the corral and said, "They'll take care of them."

Hastings wasn't so sure, but he followed Barry up the steps anyway. He almost expected Barry to just open the door and go right in, but he knocked.

The door was opened by an old man, wearing old jeans and a shirt buttoned all the way to the neck.

"It's about time," he groused.

"Is he here?" Barry asked.

"Of course he is," the old man said. He looked past Barry and scowled at Hastings. "Who's this?"

"My partner."

"Didn't know you had a partner."

"Well, I do. Can we come in?"

"Come ahead," the man said, backing away.

As they went past him, Hastings got a close-up look. He thought the man's skin looked as if he'd just spent a week in the desert. He was surprised the skin didn't crack.

The old man closed the door and then turned to face them.

"Wait here," he said. "I'll tell him you're here."

"Okay."

As the man walked away, Hastings said, "Who's that?"

"That's Dad," Barry said.

"Your dad?"

"No," Barry said, "just Dad. That's what everybody around here calls him."

"But . . . is he somebody's dad?"

"Shit, I don't know, Tracy," Barry said. "That question ain't really important, is it?"

"I guess not."

"Well, why don't we save our breath for the important questions, okay?"

"Yeah, okay, Tom," Hastings said. "Okay."

"Relax," Barry said. "You're about to get the answers to all your questions."

THIRTY-THREE

When they reached Liberty, they reined in their horses in front of the telegraph office.

"I'll be right out," Clint said.

"You think you're gonna get an answer that quick?"

"Yeah, I do."

"Fine. I'll stay with the horses."

Clint went inside. Travis looked up and down the street of the small town. He found it remarkably clean, missing most of the ruts and puddles town streets usually sported. And none of the buildings looked as if they needed repairs. Somebody was keep the carpenters in this town real busy, he thought.

He kept himself alert for trouble, but somehow he doubted that much happened on the streets of Liberty.

Clint sent his telegram, told the key operator he'd wait for the answer.

"You think it's gonna come that quick?" the middle-aged clerk asked.

"Yeah, I do."

"Suit yerself," the man said. "Seen telegrams take days to get answers, but . . . whatever you say."

Clint leaned on the counter and waited. Minutes after the key operator finished sending the message, the key began to clatter its reply.

"Sonofabitch," the man said.

He wrote down the message and handed it to Clint.

"Damndest thing I ever seed," he said.

"Thanks," Clint said.

He carried the message outside.

Travis had dismounted and was leaning against a post, holding the reins of both horses. When he saw Clint come out, he straightened up.

"So?"

"Still alive and improving," Clint said. "Also, things are going well at the saloon."

"So," Travis said, "you don't have to worry about what's goin' on back there. Only what's ahead of us."

"Right."

"So let's pick up the trail again and get this over with," Travis suggested.

"Mount up," Clint replied.

Dad knocked on the closed door and waited.

"What?" came the reply from inside.

"They're here."

"What?"

"They're here."

He waited. He heard footsteps approaching and then the door swung open. The man standing in the doorway was naked, and so was the woman on the bed behind him. He had a raging erection that was an angry red—as red as his face.

"What the hell are you bothering me for?" the man in the doorway asked.

"You wanted to know when they got here," Dad said. "They're here."

"They? Who's they?"

"That feller you hired, and his partner."

"What partner?"

"I don't know," the old man said. "He has a feller with him, and he says it's his partner."

"So it's Barry?"

"Yeah, that's what I've been tellin' you," the old man said. "He's here."

"Okay, okay," the man said. "Put them in the den, give 'em a drink, and tell 'em I'll be right there."

"Okay," the old man said, "whatever you say."

He turned to walk down the hall as the door slammed on him.

Barry and Hastings remained in the entry foyer, but they could see a lot from there. Living room to the right with expensive furniture and a dining room to the left, with a long mahogany table.

"This is a helluva house," Hastings said.

"Yep."

"How much are we gettin' paid?"

"You'll see."

"What about the four thousand?"

"We're splittin' that, too."

"Jesus," Hastings said. He was starting to see being rich in his future.

They both heard the old man coming down the stairs and fell silent.

"Come with me," he said when he reached them.

They followed him to a room he said was the "den." There was more expensive furniture, a lot of books on bookshelves, and a desk.

"He'll be right down," the old man said. "Meanwhile, do you want a drink?"

"Yeah," Hastings said, "whiskey."

"No," Barry said. "Some of that good brandy I had the last time I was here."

"All right."

The old man walked to a small bar, poured brandy from a decanter into two large snifters, and brought them to Barry and Hastings.

Hastings grabbed it, and Barry knew he was going to gulp it down.

"Don't!" he snapped.

"Whataya mean?"

"Don't gulp it down," Barry said. "You gotta sip this stuff. It's real expensive, and real good goin' down."

"Yeah?"

Barry nodded, and sipped his drink.

Hastings looked at the liquid in the glass, and then sipped it.

"Whataya think?" Barry asked.

"Yeah," Hastings said, "it's okay."

Barry nodded, sipped his again.

Hastings smelled his, sipped it again, then said, "All in all, though, I think I'd rather have a cold beer."

THIRTY-FOUR

"You're what?" Tom Barry asked, not sure he'd heard right.

"I'm not paying you," Arthur Collingswood said, pouring himself a brandy.

"Why the hell not?" Barry demanded.

Collingswood put the decanter down and turned to face the two men.

"You didn't do the job."

"Whataya talkin' about," Barry said. "I put a bullet right in his chest."

"That may be so," the man said, "but you didn't kill him."

"I took his money." Barry took the four thousand out of his saddlebag.

"How much?"

"Four thousand."

"Keep it," Collingswood said. "That's all you're going to get. He had a lot more there. You missed it."

"I looked all over."

"You panicked and ran, didn't you?" Collingswood asked. "And where are your other men?"

"They didn't make it," Barry said. "It's just us."

"Hastings, did he say your name was?"

"That's right," Hastings said. Barry had made a hasty introduction when Collingswood entered, wearing what neither Barry nor Hastings knew was called a "smoking jacket."

"Where were you when he went into Rick's Place?" the rich man asked.

"Right with him."

"And with him when he shot Hartman?"

"No," Hastings admitted. "That happened in Hartman's office. I was in the saloon."

Collingswood sipped his brandy.

"And then what happened?"

"We got out of there."

"And . . ."

"And one of our men shot the sheriff."

Collingswood looked at Barry.

"Now him you killed."

He walked around behind the desk and sat down.

"Look," Barry said, "I shot him dead center in the chest. It ain't my fault he didn't die."

"Oh? Who's fault is it, then?"

Barry didn't answer.

"And he's getting stronger," Collingswood added.

"How do you know?"

"I've got people in town. And you know what else they tell me?"

"What?" Barry asked sourly. He wished he were holding a whiskey, and not brandy.

"You've got somebody after you."

"A posse?"

Collingswood shook his head.

"One man."

Barry laughed.

"One man? So what?"

"That man is Clint Adams."

"The Gunsmith?" Hastings blurted out.

"That's right."

"What's he got to do with this?" Barry demanded.

"He and Hartman are friends," Collingswood said. "And he wants to catch whoever shot him. So you may very well have led him here."

Barry looked around, as if he'd see Clint Adams standing right behind him.

"What the hell—"

"So here's what you're going to have to do to get paid," Collingswood said.

"What?"

"You're going to have to kill the Gunsmith."

Barry and Hastings looked at each other, their mouths open.

Collingsworth laughed and said, "Bet you wish you hadn't killed your other men."

THIRTY-FIVE

They didn't have to ride very far out of town when they saw the ranch ahead of them.

"That's a big spread," Travis said.

Clint nodded. The house had two stories, the barn was huge, and there were corrals everywhere, and some outbuildings. One of those buildings looked a lot like a bunkhouse.

"A big spread," Clint said, "with a lot of men."

"Well, the tracks lead right to it," Travis said. "What do we do?"

"I think," Clint said, "we need to find out who this place belongs to."

"And then what?"

"And then send another telegram and find out if Rick knows who it is."

"So we're goin' back to town?"

Clint nodded.

"We're going back to town."

"Suits me," Travis said, turning his horse. "I could use a hot meal."

When they got back to town, they decided to play it low-key.

"We'll put up the horses and get a hotel," Clint said.

"What if Barry and Hastings leave the ranch while we're here?" Travis asked.

"I can find them again," Clint said. "Right now I want the man who hired them to shoot Rick."

"Maybe they were only hired to rob him," Travis said. "Maybe shootin' him was their own idea. Or maybe it just happened."

"Nothing just happens, Travis," Clint said. "People make things happen."

They rode to the livery, left the horses, and walked to a hotel with their saddlebags and rifles. They registered, getting a room for each of them.

Clint's original plan was to go to the sheriff's office to find out who owned the big spread outside of town, but while they were checking in, Travis said to the clerk, "We passed a real big spread ridin' into town. Who owns it?"

"Oh, that's Mr. Collingswood's place," the clerk answered. "The Rocking W."

"The Rocking W?" Travis said.

"Yeah," the young clerk said. "The brand is a W that rocks, like a rocking chair."

"Huh," Travis said.

"How long has that spread been there?" Clint asked.

"The place has been there for years, but Mr. Collingswood bought it about two years ago and really fixed the place up. He's a very rich man."

"I guess so," Travis said. "That's a heckuva place."

"It sure is."

"Why, I'll bet a man who lives in a place like that never comes to town."

"That's where you're wrong," the clerk said. "He comes to town all the time. Hell, he's on the town council."

"Is that a fact," Travis said.

"He's a very important citizen of this county," the clerk said.

"I bet," Travis said.

"Here are your keys."

"Thanks," Travis said.

"Thank you," Clint said.

They went up the stairs together, and when they got to the hall, Clint asked, "Why did you do that?"

"What?"

"Ask all those questions."

"Found out what we wanted to know, didn't we?"

"That may be so," Clint said, "but now somebody knows we've been asking."

"Well," Travis said, "I guess I didn't think of that. Still, now we know who he is. You ever hear of him?"

"Never," Clint said.

"Maybe your friend Rick has."

"Maybe," Clint said. "That's what we're going to have to find out."

They left their things in their rooms and went out to find the telegraph office.

"Can't we eat first?" Travis asked.

"I want to get this done."

As they approached the telegraph office, they spotted a café across the street.

"I tell you what," Clint said. "You go in there and get a table, order me a steak. I'll be right along."

"That suits me," Travis said. "See you there."

Clint nodded. They split up, Clint going to the telegraph office and Travis to the café.

Clint entered the office and wrote out his message. He knew he was taking a chance sending out a telegram that had the name "Collingswood" in it in a town where the man commanded such respect. But Travis had already put the word out that they were interested, so he went ahead.

The reply did not come as quickly as it had before.

"I'll be in the café across the street when the answer comes in," Clint said. He gave the clerk an extra dollar. "Will you bring it over to me?"

"Sure will, mister."

"Thanks."

Clint crossed the street to the café, found it only half filled. Travis had gotten a table in the back, so Clint joined him. There was a lot of coffee on the table, so he poured himself a cup.

"I ordered steaks," Travis said.

"Thanks."

"What's the word?"

"No answer yet."

"That worry you?" he asked. "You been getting answers pretty quick."

"I'm trying not to worry," Clint said. He sipped his coffee, made a face. "You told them to make it weak, didn't you?"

"I didn't say a word," Travis said. "That's the way they make it."

"Now I'm worried about the steaks."

"They gonna bring you an answer here?"

"Yeah."

"Then relax and eat."

Clint sat back and said, "I'm going to try."

THIRTY-SIX

They were sawing through their tough steaks with sharp knives when the telegraph clerk appeared in the door.

"Looks like your guy," Travis said.

Clint looked up and waved at the man, who hurried across the floor.

"Here's your answer, Mr. Adams."

"Thanks." He gave the young clerk another dollar.

"Yessir!"

Clint looked down at the message.

"What's it say?"

"It's not what it says," Clint said, "it's what it doesn't say."

"Huh?"

"It says not to worry, Rick is fine."

"So?"

"Why doesn't it say what the other ones said?" Clint asked.

"What do you mean?"

"This sounds like 'something happened, but don't worry, Rick is okay.'" He put the telegram down on the table, pushed his half-eaten steak away.

"You gonna eat those potatoes?" Travis asked.

"No."

"Steak's tough," Travis said, "but the potatoes are okay." He picked up Clint's plate, scraped the potatoes onto his own.

"So now you're gonna worry about this?"

"What if the whole point was to kill Rick?"

"We talked about that already."

"Yeah, we did, but if that was the point, then maybe they tried again. And I should've been there to stop it."

"You can stop it by stopping the man who's hirin' it done," Travis said. "Ain't that what we decided, too?"

"Yeah, it is." Clint pushed his chair back.

"Where you goin'?"

"I'm going to talk to the sheriff," Clint said. "Might as well find out how much help we can expect from him."

"Want me to come along?"

"No," Clint said, "that's okay, finish your potatoes . . . and mine!"

He headed for the door.

He was about to enter the sheriff's office when the door opened and a man wearing a badge started to leave. They stopped just short of bumping each other. The badge was a sheriff's star, and the man wearing it was tall, rangy, and Clint's age.

"Whoa," he said. "Sorry. You lookin' for me?"

"I am."

"Just get to town?"

"That's right."

"Well, is it important? I'm on my way—"

"It's about a man named Collingswood."

"Arthur Collingswood?"

"That's right."

The man frowned, examined Clint for a moment.

"He's an important man in this town."

"So I hear."

"So what's the Gunsmith want with Collingswood?"

"You know me?"

"I saw you once in Sante Fe. The Marlowe brothers tried to take you."

"They were young," Clint said. "That was sad."

"Yeah, it was. You want some coffee?"

"I could use some," Clint said. "I just had some in the café across from the telegraph office."

"Oh, Christ, don't eat there."

"Too late."

"Come on in, but I gotta warn you," the man said. "I make it strong."

"Suits me."

They went inside.

The sheriff introduced himself as Jack Catchings. Clint had never heard the name, but he had the feeling the man was a competent lawman.

Catchings poured some coffee, handed Clint a cup, and then sat behind his small desk. Clint sat across from him. The entire office seemed cramped.

"I know," Catchings said as if reading Clint's mind, "it's like a shoe box. I've been promised a new one."

"Promises, promises," Clint said.

"Yeah, I know." The sheriff sipped his coffee. Clint did the same. It was miles better than the café's. "Okay, so what's your business with Collingswood?"

"I think he hired some men to kill a friend of mine," Clint said.

"What makes you think that?"

"I've been tracking them," Clint said, "and they led me right to his door."

"Did you talk to him?"

"No," Clint said, "I thought I'd come and see you first."

"That was probably a good idea."

"Has he got a lot of men out there?"

"He's got a few, and they're all good with a gun."

"So this doesn't surprise you?"

"Mr. Adams," Catchings said, "when you've been a lawman as long as I have, nothing surprises you anymore. I've seen it all. A rich man using his money to get what he wants is nothing new."

"And a rich man using money to hire guns is nothing new either," Clint said. "The question is, what are you going to do about it?"

"Me?" Catching said. "What can I do? Collingswood is careful to pull all his dirty tricks away from here. He's not wanted for anything in my jurisdiction."

"Well, I tailed two men there who have committed murder," Clint said. "And they killed a lawman."

Catchings frowned.

"That does make a difference."

"I thought it might."

"What do you want to do?"

"I want to ride out there before the two men have a chance to get away."

"When?"

"As soon as possible."

"You mean . . . like now?"

"Now would suit me," Clint said.

"You got anybody with you?" Catchings asked. "A posse?"

"No," Clint said, "I've got one man with me, to watch my back."

"No posse?"

"No," Clint said, "I didn't have the time to put one together."

"So you don't have any official standing?"

"Would it make a difference if I did?" Clint asked. "I'd be out of my jurisdiction."

"Yes, you would," Catchings said, "but at least I'd be able to say I was assisting another lawman."

"Is someone going to ask you?"

"Oh, yeah," Catchings said. "The mayor will want to know. I'm afraid without some sort of official standing, I can't really—"

Clint took the sheriff's badge out of his shirt pocket and showed it to the man.

"Is this official enough?"

Catchings stared at the badge, then looked at Clint and said, "You're a sneaky sonofabitch, aren't you?"

THIRTY-SEVEN

Clint and Sheriff Catchings were walking toward the café when Travis stepped out. He stopped and waited for them to reach him.

"Travis," Clint said, "this is Sheriff Catchings."

"Sheriff."

"Mr. Travis."

"Just Travis."

The sheriff nodded.

"The sheriff is going to ride out to the Rocking W with us."

"Now?"

"Right now."

"Glad I ate, then," Travis said.

"I'll get my horse," Catchings said, "and meet you— well, right here."

"Okay," Clint said.

Catchings walked away. Clint and Travis turned and walked in the opposite direction, toward the livery.

"How'd you talk him into that?" Travis asked.

"Charm," Clint said.

"You showed him your badge, didn't you?"

"Yes, I did."

"Hey," Catchings said when Clint and Travis rode up on him, "that's some horse."

"Thanks," Travis said.

"I meant—"

"He knows what you meant," Clint said. "Don't pay any attention to him."

"We better get started," Catchings said. "It's getting late in the day."

"It's not that long a ride," Clint said.

"It is in the dark, and it's treacherous between here and there, even if you know the way."

"Okay then," Clint said, "lead on."

"Would you mind doing something for me first?" Catchings asked.

"What's that?"

"Pin that badge on."

"I'd prefer not to," Clint said. "Why?"

"I think with both of us wearing badges," Catchings said, "there's less chance that there'll be shooting. I'd feel better if you wore it."

Clint thought a moment, then said, "Okay. I'll wear it."

He took it out and pinned it on.

"Thanks," Catchings said. "I feel better now."

"I don't," Travis said. "As the only one without a badge, I guess I'll have to expect to be shot first."

"If you're really worried, I'll deputize you," Catchings said.

"Do you have an extra badge?" Clint asked.

"I have no deputies at the moment," Catchings said. "I have plenty of badges."

"No, that's okay," Travis said. "I think I'd rather not wear a badge. Let's just get going."

They rode out of town, Catchings in the lead.

Part of the way there, Travis called out for them to stop. He dismounted, made a show of checking his horse's hooves.

"Everything okay?" Clint asked.

"Give me a hand, will you?"

Clint rode back to where Travis was, while Catchings remained where he was.

"What is it?" Clint asked, dismounting.

"Take a look at this," Travis said.

Clint walked over and leaned down next to him.

"Somebody rode out to the ranch ahead of us," he said to Clint, keeping his voice down.

"How do you know?"

"Fresh trail," Travis said, "and by the stride I'd say he was movin' fast."

"Okay."

"You think the sheriff sent somebody to warn Collingswood?" Travis asked.

"I'm going to say no," Clint said. "As a rich man, he probably has men in town, watching things for him. Word probably got out that we were asking about him. Maybe even from the desk clerk."

"Am I gonna hear about that again?"

"I'm just saying, Travis," Clint said. "Maybe it was the telegraph clerk. Whatever. Look, let's just keep going, and stay alert. All right?"

"Okay."

Clint stood up and said loudly, "Should be okay."

They both mounted up and rode to where Catchings was waiting.

"Everything okay?" the lawman asked.

"Fine," Clint said.

"False alarm," Travis said.

"Then let's move," Catching said, once again taking the lead.

THIRTY-EIGHT

Collingswood's warning came barely an hour ahead of Clint, Travis, and the sheriff arriving.

"Here's your chance," he said to Barry.

"You want me to kill him here?"

"No," Collingswood said. "In town. Or on the road between here and there. I don't care where, but not here. Understand?"

"I get it," Barry said.

"Then you better get out of here before they get here." Collingswood pointed to Charlie Beck, the man who had brought him the word on the Gunsmith. "Follow Charlie back to town. He'll take you off the main road."

"Okay."

But Barry didn't move.

"What?" Collingswood asked.

"I need some money."

"Don't try to con me, Barry," Collingswood said. "You

have the four thousand you took from Rick Hartman.
Get out!"

Barry and Hastings followed Charlie Beck out the back
of the house.

Dad came into the room.

"Riders approaching."

"How many?"

"Three. Two of them are wearin' stars."

"Two?"

Dad nodded.

"Okay," Collingswood said, "tell Lewis and Watson
to stand by."

"All right. Should I arm myself?"

"Why not?" Collingswood said.

Dad nodded and left the room.

Collingswood walked to his desk, took a derringer
from the top drawer, and put it in the pocket of his smoking jacket.

Clint, Travis, and Sheriff Catchings rode up to the front
of the house. A half a dozen hands watched them from
the corral.

"None of them are armed," Clint pointed out.

"You noticed that real quick," Catchings said.

"That's how I've managed to stay alive this long," Clint
told him.

As they mounted the steps to the front door, it opened.
That was a mistake, Clint thought. It told them they were
expected.

As good as a confession.

THIRTY-NINE

The old man showed them into a den. Collingswood was seated behind a huge desk. Why, Clint wondered, did rich men always buy desks that were so big?

"Mr. Collingswood," the sheriff said.

"Sheriff," the man said. "Who are your friends?"

"This is Clint Adams," Catchings said, "and his partner, Travis."

"Clint Adams," Collingswood said. "That name is not unknown to me."

"Good," Clint said.

"What can I do for you gents?"

"I'll let Mr. Adams answer that, I think," Sheriff Catchings said.

"Very well," Collingswood said, looking at Clint. "Mr. Adams?"

"Do you know a man named Rick Hartman?" Clint asked.

"Can't say I do."

"Well, he's a friend of mine," Clint said. "He was shot recently, and I've been tracking the men who shot him."

"And?"

"And I tracked them to here."

"To Liberty?"

"No," Clint said, "to your ranch."

Collingswood frowned, looking very puzzled. He looked past them at the old man standing in the door.

"Dad, we have any killers come to the house recently?" he asked.

"No, sir."

"I didn't say they were killers," Clint said. "I only said my friend had been shot."

"Well, you've come all this way, I thought—"

"How do you know how far I've come?" Clint asked. "I never said."

Collingswood hesitated a moment, gathering his thoughts. The old man had made a mistake by opening the door too soon, and now Collingswood had made two assumptions by mistake.

"Mr. Collingswood," Clint said, "you might as well admit you hired them, because when I find them, they're going to tell me."

"I don't understand," Collingswood said. "What makes you think I hired them?"

"They'd have no reason to do it on their own," Clint said, which wasn't strictly true. It could have been personal between Barry and Rick—but according to Rick, it wasn't. "And they led me right here."

"Well," Collingswood said, "as I've told you, we have no . . . strangers here, no one who has shot anybody, no one who is running from the Gunsmith." He looked at the sheriff. "Jack, why would you even bring these men here?"

"I'm the law, Mr. Collingswood," Catchings said. "I have to check everything out."

"Well," Collingswood said, "I'll be talking to the mayor about this."

"You do that, sir," Catchings said. "but if you don't mind, I think we'll have a look around the place."

"But I do mind."

"Why?"

"Because I'm offended by your presence," Collingswood said, "and the presence of these men." He looked past them again. "Dad, show these gents out."

Catchings exchanged a glance with Clint, who gave his head a slight shake.

"Thank you for your time," Catchings said.

Clint gave Collingswood a hard look and said, "I'll see you again."

"I look forward to it," the man said.

"This way, gentlemen," Dad said.

Outside they stopped before mounting their horses.

"Two of those men by the corral are armed now," Travis said.

"I see," Clint said.

"I could have insisted he let us look around," Catchings said. "Why did you wave me off?"

"They're not in the house," Clint said. "That'd be foolish."

"The barn, then?" Travis asked.

"My bet is they're gone," Clint said, "maybe on their way to Liberty."

"I'll be able to tell," Travis said. "We just have to pick up their trail."

Clint looked at the lawman.

"When we catch them," Clint said, "they'll give him up."

"How can you be so sure?"

"Because he's arrogant," Clint said. "Once they're caught, they'll want him to be caught, too."

They mounted up.

"Travis," he said, "let's go pick up that trail."

FORTY

After riding away from the ranch house, they circled around behind it and Travis was able to pick up the trail.

"Three horses," he said, "rode away from here just recently."

"On their way to where?" the sheriff asked.

"Can't tell yet," Travis replied, "but I'd say Liberty."

"Then we better get back there."

"Let's follow the trail," Clint suggested. "Once we're sure that's where they're headed, we can get back on the main road."

"Agreed," Travis said.

They followed the trail as far as they needed to and then Travis said, "Yeah, they're definitely heading for Liberty."

"Then we better get there fast," Catchings said.

"You got any idea who might have ridden out to the Rocking W and warned them we were coming?" Clint asked.

"I have one or two ideas," Catchings said. "We can check on them when we get to town."

They suspended any further conversation and rode hard for town.

When they arrived, Clint and Travis put their horses in the livery while the sheriff took care of his own.

"Anybody come riding into town in the past hour?" Clint asked the liveryman.

"If they did, they didn't leave their horses here," the old gent said.

"Is there another livery in town?"

"Nope," he said. "If they came to town and they didn't put their horses here, then they's hidin' 'em."

"That's what I figure," Clint said. "Okay, thanks."

They left the livery and walked to the sheriff's office. Catchings had already taken care of his horse and was there, behind his desk. He looked like he was deep in thought when they entered. There was a pot of coffee on the potbellied stove.

"Coffee's not ready yet," Catchings said. "I been givin' this some thought. I come up with two fellas coulda ridden out to the Ricking W to warn Collingswood."

"Who are they?" Clint asked.

"Charlie Beck and Pete Stacker."

"What do they do?" Travis asked.

"Nothin' much, which is why they'd do anythin' for a dollar."

"So where do we find them?" Clint asked.

"Usually in a saloon."

"Okay," Clint said, "tell us what they look like and we'll split up and look."

"Pete's tall and skinny with big ears, and Charlie is half Indian, black hair, wears a bowler."

"Got that?" Clint asked Travis.

"Find one of them and then find me," Clint said. "Don't brace them alone."

"They're not dangerous," Catchings assured them.

"Maybe not, but they might have somebody dangerous with them," Clint said.

"Don't worry," Travis said, "I'll be fine."

"Do what I say, Travis, understand?" Clint said. "Not alone. Say it!"

"Okay, okay," Travis said, "not alone."

Travis left the sheriff's office. Catchings got up from behind the desk and grabbed his hat.

"We might as well all split up."

They headed for the door.

"Um, he's not your son, is he?" the sheriff asked.

"What, Travis? No. Why?"

"Well, he's young enough and . . . he kind of looks like you."

"No, he doesn't."

Catchings shrugged and said, "Suit yourself."

Outside they split up. Catchings told Clint to check the saloons; he had a few other places he could check.

"You find them," he suggested, "bring them back here and we'll question them."

"Okay."

He watched as the lawman walked away. He hoped the man was on the level, and not working for Collingswood. Rich men often had the local law in their pocket. Catchings seemed to be okay, but they were strangers, so he couldn't really count on him. Or Travis for that matter.

The only one he could trust without reservation was himself.

That was not something he ever forgot.

Tom Barry watched as Clint Adams left the sheriff's office with the lawman. They stopped just outside, exchanged a few words, and then split up.

"There," Hastings said, "he's all alone. Let's take him now."

"Wait," Barry said.

"For what?"

"Let the sheriff get far enough away," Barry said, "and then we'll take care of the Gunsmith."

FORTY-ONE

Clint remembered passing three saloons on the way into town. He didn't know which one Travis had gone to, so he just started walking. He figured he'd stop into the first one he came to.

Travis entered the Big Sky Saloon, stopped just inside the door. It was about three-quarters full, and he stood there and looked around for big ears or a bowler hat.

"Help you, cowboy?" a saloon girl asked.

She was a cute blonde, and she put her hand on Travis's arm. It was his gun arm, so he moved away slowly, so as not to insult her.

"I'm looking for Pete Stacker or Charlie Beck. Are they here?"

"No, they're not, but they usually come in."

"You haven't seen them at all today?"

"Nope, sorry. What do you want with those two drunks?" she asked.

"Just some information," Travis said.

"What kind of information can those two have?" the girl asked, rolling her eyes.

"I'll just keep lookin'," Travis said. "Thanks."

"Come on back when you're done," she said, waving at him.

"Sure," he said, and left the saloon.

Clint saw Travis coming out of the Big Sky Saloon, assumed he'd had no luck inside. He started to raise his hand to call to him when the shots rang out . . .

"Do it now," Barry said.

They had taken cover in front of the hardware store, behind some crates.

"In the back?" Hastings said.

"What'd you think, we were gonna face him?"

"Well, yeah."

"He'd kill both of us," Barry said. "Is that what you want?"

"Hell, no."

"Then kill him now." Barry drew his gun and pointed. Hastings did the same thing, and they fired . . .

The shots whizzed by Clint, just missing his ear and his shoulder. Clint had pivoted just a bit to wave at Travis, and the move had saved his life.

It also helped that Hastings's hand was shaking, and Tom Barry was just not a very good shot.

Clint rolled a second later, drawing his gun . . .

Travis heard the shots, saw Clint go down and thought he was shot. He drew his gun, looking around for the shooters. When he spotted them, he snapped off a shot in their direction, hoping it would give Clint time to find cover.

"Did we get 'im? Did we get 'im?" Hastings asked. "He went down."

"I don't know," Barry said. "Just keep shooting, goddamnit!"

Travis saw where the shots were coming from and called out to Clint.

"Clint! They're in front of the hardware store!" He pointed.

Clint nodded, waved, and turned. He motioned for Travis to stay on that side of the street, while he crossed over to the other side.

"Who's that?" Hastings said.

"I don't know."

"They spotted us. We gotta get out of here."

Barry grabbed Hastings's arm. "If you run, I'll shoot you myself. We've got a job to do."

"But—"

"You stay here," Barry said. "If we split up, we'll have a better chance."

"Where you goin'?"

"Across the street." Barry pointed his finger at Hastings. "If you run, I'll kill you."

Before Hastings could answer, Barry took off running across the street.

"Yeah," Hastings said, "you'll kill me . . . if we both survive."

FORTY-TWO

Clint saw one of the men run across the street to his side. That left him facing one, and Travis the other. The odds were even.

He moved toward the man, keeping close to the storefronts. If he could keep this one alive, he could get him to give up Collingswood.

Travis saw the same thing Clint did, that they were both down to a one-against-one situation. Keeping to the shadows as much as he could, he moved toward the hardware store.

Barry saw Clint Adams coming toward him. The situation was not going the way he had planned. He looked across the street at Hastings, who had remained behind the crates. Maybe Hastings could keep them busy while he got away.

To hell with this. What good was Collingswood's

money if he wasn't alive to spend it? Besides, he still had the four thousand.

So the man who told Hastings he'd kill him if he turned and ran . . . turned and ran.

Hastings looked across the street, saw Barry bolt and run, and cursed the man silently. The sonofabitch was leaving him to get killed.

He stood up, wanting to take a shot at Barry's fleeing back, but as he did, somebody took a shot at him.

Travis saw the man stand, thought he was going to fire at Clint, so he fired a quick shot to get his attention.

The man turned toward him, tossed his gun into the street, and put his hands in the air.

"Okay, okay," he shouted, "I'm not armed!"

Travis looked across the street, saw Clint running.

"Come on," he said to the man, "let's take a walk."

Clint saw the man start running and took off after him. If he wasn't going to stand and fight, maybe Clint could take him alive.

Barry ran to the end of the street and down an alley. He was hoping to outrun Clint, but he heard footsteps right behind him. He came to the back of the alley and found he'd run himself into a dead end. There was no way out.

He turned and grabbed for his gun.

"Don't!" Clint shouted, but it was too late. Barry, trapped and scared, panicked and kept right on going for his gun.

Clint fired twice, hitting Barry both times. Barry pulled the trigger of his gun, fired a round into the ground.

Clint ran to the fallen man, hoping to get a few words out of him.

"Damn you . . ." Barry coughed.

"You're Barry, right?"

"Fuck you."

"You shot Rick Hartman, didn't you?"

"Damn right . . . I did."

"Who put you up to it," Clint asked. "Come on, who hired you?"

Barry said, "Fuck—" and the rest was drowned out by a fountain of blood.

Clint walked back to the main street, made his way to the sheriff's office. There were no bodies in the street. Either Travis was chasing the other man, or had already taken him to the sheriff's office.

He hoped the former was true.

FORTY-THREE

As he entered the sheriff's office, he saw Travis, but not the other man or the sheriff.

"How'd it go?" Travis asked.

"He gave me no choice," Clint said. "The fool went for his gun. How about you?"

Travis crooked his finger at Clint and led him to the cell block. There was a man in one of the cells.

"Meet Tracy Hastings. Hastings, meet the Gunsmith."

The man came off the cot and grabbed the bars.

"What happened to Tom Barry?"

"He's dead."

"Good," Hastings said. "That sonofabitch told me he'd kill me if I ran, and then he did it."

"Well, he paid the price," Clint said. "So the rest is up to you."

"Whataya mean?"

"I want to know who hired you to shoot Rick Hartman," Clint said.

"Barry knew that," Hastings said. "Not me."

"Come on," Clint said, "you were both out at the Rocking W. You know Collingswood hired Barry, and Barry brought you into it."

"Then what do you need me for?"

"I need you to tell the sheriff that Collingswood hired you," Clint said.

"But . . . you're wearing a badge."

"Catchings is local," Clint said. "I'll need you to tell him."

"And then what?"

"And then he and I will go out and arrest Collingswood."

Hastings looked surprised.

"You mean it?"

"Yes."

"You'd do that?"

"I would."

"But will the local sheriff go along?"

"He will." Clint hoped he would.

Hastings gave the proposal some thought, then said, "Okay. I'll do it. Where is he?"

"He should be here any minute," Clint said.

"Do I get fed?" Hastings asked. "I ain't ate nothing all day."

"You'll get fed," Clint promised.

He and Travis walked out into the office.

"Where's the sheriff?" Travis asked.

"That's what I'm wondering," Clint said. "Maybe he found Beck or Stacker."

"We don't really need them now that we have this fella," Travis said.

"Maybe not," Clint said, "but he doesn't know that. Why don't you stay here with Hastings and I'll go and find him?"

"Suits me," Travis said. "Be careful. They tried to bushwhack you, and there may be more out there."

"I got you," Clint said. "I'll be back as soon as I can. You be careful, too."

"See you soon."

Clint left the office to go and look for Sheriff Catchings.

He went to the three saloons in town. In all three they claimed not to have seen the sheriff all night, and not to have seen either Stacker or Beck.

As he left the third saloon, he wondered how it could be true that none of the three men had been seen in any of the saloons. He was starting to have a bad feeling.

He decided to check the livery stable to see if the liveryman had seen any of the three. When he got there, the doors were open, but nobody was around. He wondered if, in this town, they left the stables open at night for late arrivals.

He went inside, took a brief look around, turned to leave, then stopped and sniffed the air. What he smelled could have been left over from the shots he had fired earlier, but he didn't think so. He turned and started looking through the stable more thoroughly. He found the body lying in the hay in one of the stalls. He was about to turn the man over when someone yelled, "Who's in here?"

Clint turned and looked at the liveryman, who entered carrying a lamp.

"Oh, it's you," he said. "You need your horse?"

"No," Clint said, "I need you to tell me who this is."
He pointed.

The man walked over and said," Jesus Christ," when
he saw the body. "Who is that?"

"I'm going to turn him over and you're going to tell
me that. Okay?"

"Sure, okay," the old man said.

Clint stepped into the stall, leaned over, and turned
the dead man over. When he saw the darkness of the
man's skin, he knew, but he stepped back and said, "Who
is it?"

"That's Charlie Beck."

"That's what I thought."

"There's his hat." The old man pointed to a corner of
the stall. What happened to him?"

"He was shot."

"I heard some shots, but I thought they were down the
street."

"They were," Clint said. "I'm betting whoever shot
Charlie used them to cover his play."

"Why would anybody wanna kill ol' Charlie?" the old
man asked.

"You live here," Clint said. "You tell me."

"He's just a drunk most of the time," the man said, "and
an errand boy."

"Errand boy for who?"

"Anybody with a dollar."

"How about a fella named Collingswood?"

The old liveryman looked surprised.

"That's a lotta dollars," the man said.

"Well," Clint said, "I better find the sheriff and let him know."

"I'll watch the body," the old man said, as if anyone would want to take it away.

Clint left the livery with a bad feeling in the pit of his stomach.

FORTY-FOUR

When he got back to the sheriff's office, Catchings was there.

"Where you been?" he asked.

"I've been looking for you," Clint said. "Everybody in the saloons said you weren't there."

"I didn't find Charlie or Pete."

"I did," Clint said. "I found Charlie—dead."

"What? Where?" Travis asked.

"How?" Catchings asked.

"He's in the livery, shot to death," Clint said. "I don't think we heard the shot over our shots."

"Somebody didn't want him to talk," Travis said.

"Sheriff," Clint said, "where were you when all the shots were being fired?"

"Other end of town, I guess," Catchings said. "Lucky you managed to take one alive."

"Yeah," Clint said, "lucky."

"What's he got to say?"

"Why don't we ask him?" Clint said. "We were waiting for you to come back."

"Let's talk to 'im, then."

Clint and Travis followed Catchings into the cell block. Clint watched Hastings closely to see if he recognized Catchings when they walked in, but his face didn't show any sign of it.

"You're in a lot of trouble, my friend," the sheriff said. "Tryin' to shoot a man in the back is as cowardly as it gets."

Clint wondered how Catchings knew they'd tried to shoot him in the back if he was at the other end of town when the shooting took place.

"That was Barry's idea," Hastings said, "not mine."

"And you just wanted to face the Gunsmith? Is that it?" Travis asked.

"I didn't wanna have nothin' to do with him, but . . ." Hastings let it trail off.

"But what?"

"There was too much money involved."

"How much?" Clint asked.

"Well, I don't know. Barry wouldn't tell me. But he said we were gonna get paid a lot."

"Okay," Clint said, "so who was going to pay you all this money?"

"Some rich fella named Collingswood," Hastings said, "has a ranch just outside of town." Clint looked at the sheriff and said, "You need anything else?"

"Nope," Catchings said. "Let's ride out there and get him."

Catchings wanted Travis to stay behind with Hastings, but he refused. When he suggested waiting until morning, instead of riding out there in the dark, Clint refused. So the three of them mounted up and rode out to the ranch.

Clint and Travis had a few minutes to talk while the sheriff fetched his horse.

"What do you think?" Travis asked.

"I don't trust Catchings," Clint said. "How did he know they tried to shoot me in the back if he was at the other end of town, as he claims? And he sure wanted you to stay behind."

"And get you out to the ranch alone," Travis said.

"This may get bloody," Clint said.

"I'm ready."

When Catchings joined them, they quieted down and rode out to the ranch in silence.

Just before they reached the ranch, Catchings held up his hand and reined in.

"When we go in, you better let me do the talking," he told them.

"What talkin'?" Travis asked. "We're gonna arrest him, right?"

"We gotta do it right," Catchings said. "I don't want the mayor to be able to cut him loose."

"You can start out doing the talking," Clint said, "but if it starts to go bad, I'm stepping in. I'm not letting this man get away."

The sheriff began to speak, but Clint didn't wait. He started for the ranch at a gallop.

"Three riders," Dad said, sticking his head into Collingswood's den.

"Who?"

"It's too dark to tell."

"Three," Collingswood said. "It could be the sheriff with Barry and Hastings."

"If they killed the Gunsmith," Dad said. "If not, it could be the sheriff with Adams and that other fella."

"You're right," Collingswood said. "Get Watson and Lewis."

"Right."

"And arm yourself, Dad."

"Right."

The old man left the room. Instead of putting a derringer into his pocket, Collingswood took a Colt from his desk. He stuck it in his belt, then closed his smoking jacket over it.

FORTY-FIVE

When they knocked on the front door, it was Dad who opened it again.

"Gentlemen," he said, "it's late."

"We're here to see your boss," Catchings said.

"As I said—"

Clint brushed by Dad into the house. As he did so, he could tell the old man was armed.

"Adams—" Catchings said, following him.

Travis brought up the rear.

Clint remembered the way to the den and headed there. As he entered the room, Collingswood looked up. He must have been disappointed to see Clint, but he kept it off his face.

"Mr. Adams—"

"Stand up, Collingswood!"

"I don't understand."

"You're under arrest."

"This is ridiculous. I—"

Clint reached over the desk, grabbed the man by the front of his smoking jacket, and pulled him across. As he did, the jacket came open and he saw the gun. He grabbed it, disarming the man.

When Catchings entered the room, Collingswood was pretty much dangling from Clint's clenched hands.

"Adams! Damn it!"

"You better do something, Catchings!" Collingswood warned.

"Yes, Sheriff," Clint said, "it's time to declare yourself. Unless you already did that by killing Charlie Beck."

"Sheriff," Collingswood said, "I'll have more than just your badge!"

Clint shook Collingswood, forcing him to quiet down.

"Hastings gave you up, Collingswood. You paid them to rob and shoot Rick Hartman. Maybe you even wanted him killed, but they didn't get the job done. So you sent them after me. Now Barry's dead, and Hastings is in jail. Which is where you're going."

Collingswood gave Catchings a hard look.

"He's right," Catchings said.

"Well, then do something," Collingswood said. "What do I pay you for?"

Travis was behind Catchings, waiting to see if he was going to have to make a move.

Clint looked at Catchings.

"I'm taking him out of here," he said. "You going to try and stop me?"

Catchings raised his hands and stepped back.

"Travis, clear the way down the hall. The old man has a gun."

"He's harmless," Collingswood said. "Don't hurt him."

They made their way along the hall with Travis in front, Catchings behind them. Clint moved sideways, in order to keep his eye on the sheriff.

When they got to the entry foyer, there was nobody there.

"Now what?" Travis asked.

"We're going outside," Clint said.

"They'll be out there," Travis told him.

"I know."

"Should I go out the back—"

"No," Clint said, "let's just go on out. We can count on Mr. Collingswood to keep us safe."

"I hope you're right."

"Open the door and then get behind me. Watch our friend the sheriff."

"Hey, now look—"

"Open it."

Travis opened the door, then stepped aside so Clint could push Collingswood out first.

FORTY-SIX

They stepped out onto the porch. At the foot of the steps were five men, all armed.

"You better tell your men to back off," Clint said to Collingswood.

"Why should I?"

"Because you'll get the first bullet."

"If you take me to town, you'll put me in jail," the man said, "or put a bullet in my back and claim I was escaping. No, I think I'll take my chances here." He looked down at his men. "Watson! If he tries to take me away, start shooting."

"Yes, sir."

Clint heard something off to his left, turned, and saw the old man, Dad, brandishing a gun. He didn't move, but Travis drew and fired. The old man folded in half, and slumped to the floor of the porch.

"Dad!" Collingswood said. "You sonofabitch, you killed my father!"

"Take it easy," Clint told Travis. "You didn't have to—"

"Get them!" Collingswood shouted. "Get them now!"

Clint reacted immediately. He pushed Collingswood down the stairs then went flying toward his men, who were in the act of drawing their guns. If they had fired, they would have hit him.

They had to duck to the side to avoid him. That gave Clint and Travis the time they needed.

Travis's gun was already out, so he simply started shooting.

Clint drew and began to fire with deadly accuracy. It was all over in a few minutes. The five ranch hands were down and not moving. Collingswood was on the ground, looking around with a stunned expression on his face.

Clint was reloading when Collingswood's eyes fell on a gun that was lying near him.

"Don't do it—" Clint said, but he was cut off by a shot from behind him. A bullet struck Collingswood, who stiffened, and then slumped.

Clint turned, expecting to see that Travis had fired the shot, but instead it was Sheriff Catchings who'd done it.

"He was going for that gun," Catchings said.

"You shot him to shut him up," Clint said.

"About what?"

"About you working for him," Clint said.

"That's silly."

Travis was moving in among the bodies.

"They're all dead."

"Self-defense," Catchings said. "There won't be any trouble."

"Not for us," Clint said, "but there will be for you."

"What do you mean?"

"You killed Beck."

"I didn't," Catchings said. "I didn't even know he was dead until you said so. Collingswood probably had him killed."

"Yeah," Travis said, "by you."

Catchings looked at Travis, then back at Clint.

"You can't prove that," Catchings said. "In fact, it's my job to find who did kill him."

Clint looked around, saw some of the other hands coming up to the house to see what had happened. None of them were armed.

"We better get back to town," Clint said.

"Yeah," Catchings said, "we can settle this back in town. And I can have somebody come back for the bodies."

"What happened, Sheriff?" somebody asked.

They went down the steps, stopped at their horses. The sheriff told the hands to cover the bodies, but not to move any. He'd have somebody come and pick them up. He also told them he thought they were all out of work.

"What are we gonna do?" Travis asked.

"Let the sheriff think he's gotten away with everything," Clint said. "When we leave, we can send a federal marshal back to look into him. We did what we came to do."

"Okay," Travis said.

"But just in case," Clint said, "we'll keep watching each other's backs."

FORTY-SEVEN

Several weeks later Rick Hartman walked into Rick's Place in the morning. Clint was sitting there having breakfast with Travis and Delia.

"There he is," Clint said. "Walking upright."

Rick walked to the table and sat down. Cable, the new bartender, who was getting good at the job, asked Rick, "You want some breakfast?"

Rick turned and said, "Cable, is that you? Yeah, sure, bring me some eggs."

"Comin' up, boss."

Rick looked around.

"Surprised the place didn't fall down without you?" Clint asked.

"Actually, I am," Rick said.

"Well, Delia and the girls did a great job while you and me were gone."

"Sounds like somebody deserves a raise," Rick said, looking at Delia.

"And maybe a promotion?" she asked.

"Don't push it," Rick said.

She laughed.

Rick looked at Clint.

"I guess I owe you a lot."

"You owe me nothing," Clint said. "I only did what I had to do."

"Killing Collingswood was a big favor," Rick said. "Years ago we were partners, but I had to walk away from him because he was amoral. I guess it took him this long to make enough money to come after me."

"Well," Clint said, "it wasn't enough."

"Only because of you, brother," Rick said.

Cable brought out Rick's breakfast at that point. Clint stood up and walked to the bar to pour himself some more coffee. Travis joined him.

"So what now?" he asked as Clint poured him a cup of coffee, too.

"I'm going to rest here awhile and then move on," Clint said. "Are you going to keep following me?"

"No," Travis said, "I think I'm done with that."

"So what's next for you?"

Travis looked at Clint and said, "I guess I gotta come clean at some point, huh?"

"I was hoping," Clint said.

"The best way to do this," Travis said, "would be for you to meet me in the street."

Clint stared at him, then said, "You're kidding, right?"

"No," Travis said. "The turning point came when that old man had the drop on you and you didn't fire. I had to kill him. That's when I knew I could take you."

"I didn't kill the old man because he was no danger," Clint said. "He wasn't going to shoot."

"I think he was," Travis said.

Clint continued to stare at the young man.

"Why are you so shocked?" Travis asked. "I kept you under surveillance for a few months, then rode with you on a mission."

"And it was all because you were trying to figure out when to kill me?"

"What else?"

"Well, at one point I thought we were really getting along."

"We were," Travis said. "And we'd probably be friends if you hadn't killed my mother."

"What?"

"My mother," Travis explained. "It's very simple. Fifteen years ago you killed my father. Six months later, distraught, my mother died."

"So you're saying you want to kill me because I killed your father?"

"No," Travis said, "my father was a sonofabitch, but my mother loved him, and couldn't live without him. So . . . you killed my mother."

"That logic is . . . 'faulty' doesn't even say it."

Travis stared at Clint and said, "The time has come. I'll meet you outside."

Clint stared into Travis's eyes and saw a young man he had not seen before. A disturbed young man.

"Travis . . . what were your mother's and father's names?"

"It doesn't matter what their names were, or if you

even remember them," Travis said. "The fact remains you killed them." With that, the young man turned and walked out the batwing doors.

Clint went back to the table, where Rick asked, "Where's he going?"

"To wait for me in the street."

"What?" Delia asked.

"That's what I said. Apparently, he says I killed his parents, and now he wants to kill me." "Why didn't he say anything or try anything before now?" Rick asked.

"Again, apparently he was studying me."

"And he's decided now is the time?" she asked.

"Yes."

She studied him for a moment, then said, "Okay, either he's kidding, or you are."

"I'm afraid not," he said.

"What are you going to do, Clint?" she asked.

"What can I do?" Clint asked. "Whenever I go out, he'll be there."

"Can't you just walk away?"

"It's not that simple, Delia."

"This is Clint's life, Delia," Rick said. "He can't escape it."

"But . . . what if he kills you?" she asked.

"He can't," Clint said.

"Why do you say that?"

"I've seen him use a gun," Clint said, adjusting his holster on his hips. "He doesn't have a chance."

Watch for

VENGEANCE RIDE

386th novel in the exciting GUNSMITH series
from Jove

Coming in February!

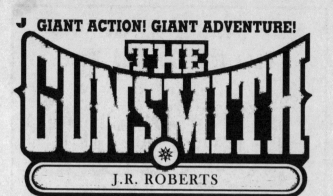

J GIANT ACTION! GIANT ADVENTURE!

THE GUNSMITH

J.R. ROBERTS

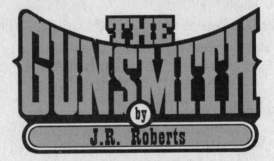